Only Lovers Wear Sunlight

Only Lovers Wear Sunlight

Short Stories Celebrating Life and Yearning

Nick Viggiano

iUniverse, Inc.
Bloomington

Only Lovers Wear Sunlight
Short Stories Celebrating Life and Yearning

iUniverse books may be ordered through booksellers or by contacting:

iUniverse
1663 Liberty Drive
Bloomington, IN 47403
www.iuniverse.com
1-800-Authors (1-800-288-4677)

ISBN: 978-1-4620-4387-3 (sc)
ISBN: 978-1-4620-4389-7 (hc)
ISBN: 978-1-4620-4388-0 (ebk)

Printed in the United States of America

iUniverse rev. date: 07/28/2011

Contents

Happy New Year

Her mother was right. It was a very ugly house. The paint was peeling, the steps were cracked, even the trees in the yard drooped sadly. Krista Starling considered all this as she opened the front door with her new key. All those critical comments from all those well-meaning people . . . Had she made a mistake? But as she closed the door and ran up the stairs to *her* apartment, that feeling returned.

All it took was one breath of the freshly painted walls, or one look at the sketches she finally had room to hang, or one listen to the music she could play at any time, or her feet touching the cold floor of her own bathroom, or her clothes lying anywhere she wanted to leave them. Krista. Krista. Krista. She was in control of it all. No one else. No one could stop her. She did a little dance. She was happy.

Living one floor below was an older couple, Peter and Paula Thompson, who had been in the same apartment for twenty-two years.

"Do you hear that?" Paula Thompson yelled to her husband.

"Hear what? I'm watching TV," Peter replied.

"Do you hear that noise she's making?"

"I don't hear anything."

"You're just saying that because you saw her outside yesterday, and she's a good looking young girl. You like her, and you think she'll like you. That's why you pretend you don't hear anything!."

"Oh, leave her alone," Peter said between bites of his favorite double chocolate cookies. "She's just starting out. Weren't you just starting out once?"

"No. I never got a start. I married you."

"All the same. She seems nice. She has a job. She goes to bed early. What more do you want?"

"For now. As soon as she settles in she'll be having wild parties. I can tell by the way she dresses. She's one of those girls. Already I don't like her."

Krista had already met the other inhabitants of the house. Old John on the first floor, he had trouble breathing. Maybe she could go to the store for him when it was too warm or too cold outside. Mr. Thompson seemed very nice. He wanted to know all about her, but his wife made a grumpy face at her and barely said hello.

This was the beginning. Her birth had been a false beginning. The first twenty-two years had been spent in limbo, always under a watchful eye, always under the thumb, suffocating in love without one bit of understanding.

None of that mattered anymore. She was free to live and think like an intelligent being, free to read and write and sing and love—who would her lover be in this brand new world? How would she choose him? How long would it take? How often would he stay with her? Would he wake early and kiss her shoulder as he left? Or would he sleep all day and then eat all her food after she had gone? As long as he held her and kissed her and kissed her again. She liked being kissed on the neck. And on her shoulders. And down her back . . .

Someone was ringing her bell. Perhaps it was him. Lovers meet many different ways. As she ran down the stairs, she pictured him. She was breathing hard. She brushed some cookie crumbs from her sweater as she opened the door, but it was only her uncle.

"Hi, Uncle Bob."

"Hello, dearie. Hope I'm not intruding. I thought I'd come and see the new place and wish you good luck."

"That's so sweet. Come on in."

The old man's shoes squeaked. He climbed slowly, putting one foot on a step, then drawing the other one up for a short break before attempting the next step, until he finally arrived at the top. "Here, Uncle Bob, let me take that bag for you."

"I just brought you a few housewarming gifts."

"You really shouldn't have."

"I'm an old man with no one to spend his money on. And you only move into a first apartment once. I remember my first new apartment . . ."

"Uncle Bob, let's get inside, and then you can tell me."

Krista took his coat and hat and sat him on her new sofa. She came out of the kitchen with a glass of lemonade.

"This is a lot fancier than my first place. I had a chair and a table and a tiny bed. It was just one room. And I shared it with the mice. They ate better than I did. You're making enough money, aren't you? When I had that place, I only had money to go to the movies once a week. If it was a bad film, you were stuck."

"I'm making enough money," Krista smiled at him. He was a sweet old man.

"Okay. Look at what's in the bag."

She placed the bag between them, reached in, and pulled out frozen meat.

"I know you like to cook. But you eat all those vegetables and rice. You need red meat once in a while."

"Thanks."

The other item in the bag wasn't food but a pair of pajamas, with feet.

"Sometimes these places don't have good heat. You need to keep your feet warm. Remember that. A lot of body heat comes out through your feet."

"Thanks, Uncle Bob." She gave him a kiss.

"Yeah, I like this place." He put his glasses on to get a better look. "You know, you've got a lot of people wantin' you to do well. The whole family's proud of you, even if they don't say it."

"I know."

"They're just concerned about you being alone. Me too. Don't you know any nice Italian boys?"

"Why does he have to be Italian?"

"Well, it would really please your grandmother if you married a nice Italian boy. Or even a not so nice one. She'd still be happy. But I'm thinking of you. You don't want to stay alone for too long. It's nice at first. But you don't want to live your life like this."

"There are many things that I want to do. If a man happens to come along and involve himself in my life, then that's great too."

"Well, a woman can only do so much alone. Even an intelligent one like you."

"But if I were a man, everything would be okay?"

"If you were a man, we'd want to see you get married too. It's always easier to go through life together. I don't know what I would have done if it weren't for your aunt. Of course, she was a terrible cook. And she drove like a maniac. I wouldn't let her drive my car. I wouldn't even let her park it. And her feet always smelled. When she took her shoes off at night, oh, the stink! I told her to get some of them odor-eaters. But you think she would listen? She was a stubborn woman. Never agreed with me. But did I argue? No. Because I knew it was better to have a stubborn, hard-headed, feet-smellin', short and plain-lookin' woman than to have none at all."

Krista loved her uncle, but his stories and experiences didn't help her at all.

"Well, honey, I've taken up too much of your time. You've probably got a lot of things to do to get settled in here."

"Do you want to stay for dinner? I'll make something . . . Maybe I could cook the meat."

"No. No. You've got a lot to do, I know. You're just trying to be nice to an old man. I just wanted to wish you luck. Make sure you didn't starve. Do you have good heat here?"

"The heat's fine."

"That's good. That's good." Uncle Bob began to rise. It took him a bit to straighten himself from the sitting position. "Now remember, honey, if you ever think you want to take me up on that job offer, it's still open. I have the money. I could set you up in business. Everything you need. You would run the whole show. I would just be in the background."

"That's sweet of you, but I have many things I want to do."

"You would be good in business. You have a good head on your shoulders."

"It would look funny anyplace else, wouldn't it?"

The old man laughed and gave her a kiss.

"Don't walk me down. I'm not that old."

"You'll be okay getting to your car?"

"I'll be fine, dear. If you need anything, you'll call me. Right?"

"Yes. But I really don't need anything."

As she watched him pull away she realized he hadn't heard the last of what she said. Who did listen to her? No one in her family. They were all certain about what they wanted her to be. If any one of them had only stopped to hear her when she spoke with her true voice! She had tried to tell them. She tried many times to show what was inside. Did anyone ever notice? They had already taken that photograph and planted it right behind their eyes, the one that showed her exactly as they wanted to see her. They'd never take the time to form another picture, no matter what she did.

But what of all the people she had yet to meet? They had no image. She would be free to show her true self. It was so heavy, the outer shell she had to carry around. In this new life perhaps she could just be who she was, Krista—interested in all things creative, wanting to read and learn everything and travel everywhere, using all her senses and feeling exhilarated instead of bored by the silliness and stupidity that had previously surrounded her. It made her anxious to bring on whatever was to come. With all of these new people soon to be entering her life, the apartment would have to be spotless, plants watered and in their proper places, color-coordinated towels and soaps in the bathroom, books and music in alphabetical order. What if it happened before she was ready? How would it start? Would it be just like she thought? What did she need to do? She walked to the window and leaned her head against the glass. The trees weren't dying. They just needed a bit of care.

She was afraid to open her eyes. Not another one, not another gray, cold, miserable day. Lately they had all been the same. Depressing weather, demoralizing job, and then home to an empty apartment. She knew it was only temporary. She knew it had to change. Why did it affect her so? Krista Starling was better than that. She could rise above the impermanent. Everything changes. *Think of your poetry. Think of the future. Clouds will turn to sun, and jealous co-workers will be left behind.*

She opened one eye and then the other. The day was bright, and for a moment she felt like a child. She bounced up and out of bed and left all that was troubling her between the sheets and the blankets.

Saturday. Sunshine. A meeting with her friend Maria. This would be a good day. She opened the window, and a gust of wind made her shiver. Cold and alone. Wait—no sadness on this day. As she shut the window, a song came into her head.

Krista was brushing her teeth when she heard a familiar horn in the driveway. She waved out the window and held up two fingers, meaning it would be at least fifteen minutes before she could possibly be ready. The beeping continued at two-minute intervals until she finally locked the front door and ran to the car.

"Right on time, as usual." Maria shook her head.

"What's up, girlfriend?" Krista got into the car and adjusted the seat to her liking.

"Do you own an alarm? You can program your phone, you know."

"It's Saturday. Day of rest, day of leisure. Remember? Let's go have some fun."

"It's a good thing I'm so understanding."

"It's a good thing. For sure. I'm so impressed. Where are we going?"

"I thought we'd go to the park. Take a walk. Look at the trees. Nature stuff."

"Good one. Then after that we could get something to eat."

"Can't we do anything without it involving food?'

"A girl's gotta eat, as long as you're paying."

Maria laughed. Krista could make people forget whatever it was about her that annoyed them. She was easy to be with. Everyone said so. That's why she couldn't understand why it was so difficult to find someone . . . *Don't think of it now. Keep your mind clear. Stay in the present. Stay on course. Stay within yourself.* So many things to remember.

"We're here."

The two young women got out of the car and began to walk. Of all the people hiking in the woods that day, not one was dressed like Maria. If there was such a style as Lumberjack Chic, she embodied it. It would be at most a two-mile jaunt through the forest, but one had to look good.

Krista's wardrobe cost much less, but it could be said that she was still more attractive. She had a simplicity, something natural, a grace that enhanced all her features. Her smile was radiant, and her red hair sparkled in the sunshine.

"I'm so frustrated," Maria said as dead leaves crackled under their boots. "My laptop's not working again. I just took it in to get repaired, and they did something to it. I don't know what they did, but now it's not working again. I'm so mad!"

"Do you ever get the feeling that we rely too much on technology?"

"There's no other way to do it. How could I survive without my laptop? What would I do? All my information is in there. Everything. For work and other things. If I had to put that all on paper, if I had to write it down, it would take forever."

Maria brushed back her hair.

"I'm glad I don't have to depend on any of those gadgets."

"You should get a laptop. I can't believe you still don't have one. You could write your poetry and stories on it. It would save you so much time."

"Just because it's easier, doesn't mean it's better. Just because it's easier to write on a computer, doesn't mean the writing is better."

"Everybody writes on a computer, even people who live on islands. You're probably the only one left who uses a pen."

"No. There are others. I saw a man on the train the other day writing something in a notebook."

"How old was he? Ninety? You need to join the twenty-first century. Don't make it so hard on yourself. Why do you think you can't find anyone to go out with?"

Some of the trees were already bare, their branches extending up like withered arms in prayer. Others still held onto their reds and yellows and oranges, fighting the wind and the inevitable gloom of lifeless winter.

For the first time during their walk, Krista felt the cold air. She had the sense that she was alone, frozen, apart, as unprotected as the naked trees. They at least had the memory of summer to keep them warm. How fortunate. How lucky.

Maria's voice interrupted her gloomy thoughts. "I had the best dinner ever at that restaurant we went to the other night. You know my friend Veronica? She kept talking about this place and how good it was, and every time I talked to her, she kept saying we should go there. So last Friday night we finally did. They have the best seafood, and all the waiters wear black and their pants are really tight."

"That's a good reason to go there."

"It is!" Maria insisted. "Who wants to be served by unattractive people? That would ruin my appetite. Give me a nice young waiter with tight black pants, and I'll eat anything he brings me."

"I'll bet you would."

"We're going back again next week. You should come. Maybe you'll see something you like."

"I like seafood."

"Of course you would just go for the food, Miss Looking for the Perfect Mate. You gotta break out, girl. Stop dreaming. Everything's not like a movie. You have to get out and meet all different sorts of guys. Forget about the perfect one. Where is he? Have some fun. Don't worry about whether it's love or not. You'll spend a lot of time alone in your room if you do." Maria stopped to fix her hair again. "This wind is driving me crazy,"

I'm not looking for perfect, Krista assured herself. *Far from it. Just the opposite.* She would give anyone a chance. She was open to any experience, to all possibilities. She would talk to anyone. She smiled at everyone she saw on the street. She was ready. What were these men waiting for?

Again, Maria's voice dragged her back to the present. "Hey, why don't we go away for a few days? I would love to just lie on a beach and do nothing. I could wear that new bikini I bought. You should see how small it is. It's sinful."

"I don't know. I guess I could read on the beach."

"Read? On a beach with gorgeous men all around? Krista, you really need to stop going to those bookstores and start going somewhere where you'll meet someone."

"There are men who like to read, and they go to bookstores."

"Yeah. They're called geeks. Or else they're gay."

"And what scientific study did you consult to obtain this data?"

"Either that or they're the 'shy guy.'"

"Shy men are sweet. They're polite. They're usually intelligent. They listen to what you say. They like to hold hands. They like to walk in the park. They'll kiss you when no one's looking. They'll buy you flowers on your birthday. They don't mind when you're a little bit late, they're just so happy that you didn't forget them. They laugh at your jokes. Sometimes they write you poems. Maybe they're bad, awful poems, but it doesn't matter. They never yell. They never complain about trivial matters. They're always appreciative and attentive . . ."

Krista kept talking, but not for her friend's benefit. She closed her eyes. For a moment she couldn't feel the cold.

"Hey, Cinderella. Wake up." Maria was tapping her on the head. "I hope you had a good time on that planet you were visiting. Because here on Earth, it's not like that. If your head's always full of dreams, you'll never meet anyone."

"What would we be without our dreams?"

"Happier. Dreams just lead to false expectations. You can never fulfill them. But real life is right out there. Real live people. Live men with beautiful bodies and sexy mouths and gentle hands. So many of them, ready and willing and waiting. Even for you. You could find someone easily. It's so easy. Men are so easy. All you've gotta do is change your thinking. Enter the real world. If you come out with me, I guarantee you'll meet someone."

"Yeah, but will he be worth meeting?"

"Is he a man? Does he have two legs and something between those legs? Then he's worth meeting."

"It's all so, I don't know, it all sounds so crass and mechanical."

"Yeah, and you just have to hope his mechanics are in good working order. Sometimes they need a little lube, a little polishing . . ."

Maria was lost in pleasant thoughts of her own. Krista looked up through the trees at the fading sunlight. Each sunset marked another day lost. The passage of time supposedly brings wisdom. Instead her mind seemed to be filled only with confusion. So many thoughts—which to follow? So many images—were they all illusions?

Those who are successful are the ones who never lose sight of the goal. Those dreams, they weren't illusions, they were essential. She must keep them alive. Focus. Intense focus. She must eliminate unnecessary thoughts, cut out all distractions.

"Have you ever seen that show on TV where the women have babies, and they didn't even know they were pregnant?"

"No," Krista said.

"Talk about stupid. Who would watch something like that?"

"It looks like you did."

"Only twice. There're a few shows that I like. I watch them before I go to bed. They make me laugh, and I forget about what went on during the day. I don't like to think at night."

"It's good to relax."

"I used to read before I went to bed, but then I would have to think about and try to understand what I read, and it hurt my head. I can't remember the last time I read a book except for work. Oh, I know, it was that one about the vampires who go to a small town and pretend they're social workers, and then they suck the blood out of all the teenagers and turn the parents into zombies. I think it was called *I'm Dead and So Are You.*"

"Sounds interesting."

"But after I read it I kept having nightmares. People chasing me. With big teeth. Every night. So I never did read the sequel. I never got to find out what happened to all the characters. The first book ended with the vampires taking over the high school cafeteria, and the special lunch of the day was Teacher's Brains."

"Maybe you could read it during the day when the sun is out, because the sunshine destroys the power of the vampire. Then you could tell me what happens."

"I could lend you the first book if you want it."

"Oh, I can't. Not right now. I have so much to read. It would just sit there for months before I could get to it. But thank you anyway. I'll let you know when I'm ready."

Maria had to stop talking so she could apply protective lip gloss. "Maybe you could lend me one of the books you're reading when you're done with it, and then we could discuss it. That would be fun. But not any of that Russian literature that you read. Too depressing. And the books are so big. And why do they all have so many names?"

"There are short works of Russian literature too."

"I like reading cookbooks. Maybe we could each find a recipe. We could make it and have dinner."

"That sounds like fun."

"I know. We could have a dinner where we each eat what the other person cooked and then discuss a book during dessert."

"You don't want to do too many things at one time."

"Oh, I forgot to tell you, there's this other book I'm dying to read about two people who are shipwrecked on an island. They come upon this tribe in the forest who normally eat strangers, but because the man and the woman castaways are such good singers, they teach the tribe to sing instead of eating them. They form an opera company and eventually get rescued and take the tribe back to America with them, and they tour all over the world as the only totally native opera company. It's called *Don't Die, Fledermaus, Live.*"

"That's a bestseller, is it?"

"Yeah. Everyone I work with has read it. Shh. Look. Here come those two guys we passed on the way up."

Maria was practiced at the art of appearing not to be interested while showing she was. The two men smiled as they passed. Maria elbowed Krista.

"Why didn't you say something?"

"What should I say? 'Hi, fellas. I'm one hot single woman with her own apartment just waiting for one of you hunky guys to come back to my place and show me a good time.'"

"That's it. That's it exactly. You have to speak up. How will they know you're alive if you don't say anything?"

"How will they know I'm alive? How does anyone know I'm alive? That's the question."

"Huh?"

They had arrived back at the car.

"Nothing. I said nothing." *I always say nothing,* Krista thought. *I don't know how to speak my mind. Who would I tell my thoughts to, anyway? Who would listen? The best conversations I have are with myself. How sad is that? I have so many things to say to that one person. I go over and over them in my head. What if I never get the chance? What if it will all have to stay inside? I will burst. That can't happen. That will never happen. This feeling is only temporary. How long?*

The snow fell in large, soft flakes. Krista tried again and again to catch one on her tongue, but her nose kept getting in the way. She spun around and opened her eyes. It took winter to make the trees beautiful. She shivered without a coat as she ran back inside and up the stairs.

It was so quiet. The constant stream of vehicles on the highway and planes up above had almost vanished. She could take in the scene without interruption, count the snowflakes, watch them land, losing themselves among the others. But before long she couldn't see them at all. She thought of the cold, the months of cold and ice. No sun. Always gray. The constant bundling and unbundling just to stay alive. Fighting the wind. People hard and stiff, closed against the weather. Don't want to talk. Never smile. Walk right by. No one to meet. No chance to warm her hand in someone else's. No sweetness. No comforting. No long nights together before the fire. No soft caress in bed. No kiss behind the ear in the morning. Everything cold. Empty.

Dark. Sullen. Devoid of life. Devoid of meaning. Devoid of love.

She was shivering still. She got into bed and pulled the blanket up over her. Blessed are those who have someone to warm them.

It didn't take long for her to drift into that state where soon she would be dreaming of something better. Then the bell rang. She jumped. Oh no, the parents. They were coming for dinner. Even the snow couldn't keep them away.

Krista ran down the stairs and opened the door. Her mother was standing there, pouting, wearing a floppy hat with a peacock feather sticking straight up in the air. Her father kicked at the steps repeatedly to remove the snow from his shoes.

"Krista, what took you so long? We're freezing out here. Your father didn't even wear his boots. I told him his feet would be cold."

"I'll be fine when we get inside."

"Did you forget we were coming, dear? I called three times this week to remind you."

"No, Mom, I didn't forget," Krista replied, always polite. "Come on in. It's nice and warm upstairs."

They walked up, her father holding two shopping bags.

"Do you ever see your neighbors? I haven't seen them yet."

"They keep to themselves, Dad."

"Not like when I was a kid. You'd say hello to everyone as you walked down the street. The parents looked out for all the kids, and you'd visit on holidays and birthdays, and all . . ."

"That was quite a long time ago, dear."

"Why do you take pleasure in reminding me how old I am?"

"Well, you're the one who is always telling those stories, the same old stories. We've all heard them before, haven't we, Krista?"

"Maybe we should go in." Krista nudged them inside and closed the door.

"Oh, I see you've changed the curtains, dear. That's a much better color. That other set made it look like a bordello."

"Yep. That's what I'm running here, Mom. You guessed it. That's how I make my money."

"Don't joke, dear. Many of us are but one step away from a life of misfortune and misery."

"Speak for yourself." Krista's father sat on the sofa and took off his shoes.

Her mother began the inspection room by room.

"You've done a nice job with the place, dear. I hope you'll be able to keep it."

"I do work, Mom. I make money."

"It's so expensive for a woman to live on her own. So many bills. And unexpected events. And what about your health? Have you been to the dentist? There are so many diseases you could catch. Your teeth are very important. I'll make an appointment."

"Yes, Mom, I've been to the doctor, the dentist, the podiatrist, the chiropractor. I've had acupuncture, aromatherapy, Chinese massage, spiritual cleansing. I've had the swine flu shot, the chicken flu shot, the green monkey flu shot, and a shot of Jack Daniels. I've got it covered."

"Wow, if you can afford all that you must be doing okay," her father said. "Do you mind if I eat some of these nuts?"

"Well, they are for the guests, but I guess it's okay."

Krista was busy in the kitchen preparing the first course. Her mother emerged from the bathroom.

"I like the guest soaps you have in the bathroom, dear. So, do you have a lot of guests?"

"And by guests I assume you mean men."

"They could be men or women. I'm sure you've had your friends over to see the place."

"Even though you think I'm running a bordello, no, I don't have men staying over every night."

"I know it's the twenty-first century, but a woman should still behave properly. All those shows on television with all those disgusting girls, I don't understand it. People live like trash. They can't speak, they can't think, they can't read. They don't learn anything in school, their parents teach them nothing, and then they try to get a job, and they can't fill out the application. They walk around with everything showing. What happened to manners? There was a young woman in the store the other . . ."

"Mom, why do you even pay attention to that? It has nothing to do with you."

"This is our country, Krista. This is our society. And this is what it's coming to? Every day I have to encounter these people. Why should I have to put up with it? What have I done? I've worked, I've had respect, and I've lived the right way. Why should I have to watch it all fall apart?"

"It's silly to get so upset."

"That's what I say," said a voice from the living room. "Why get upset?"

"Because it's not right. Neither of you understand. But that's okay. It's my fault because I'm old and stupid."

"Who said that? Nobody said that. You just can't let these things bother you. Go and sit down, and I'll bring in the salad."

"No, I'm sorry, dear. But I don't feel like eating now." Her hands were fluttering. To calm them she kept smoothing her dress and fixing her hair.

"Mom, it's all right. Your hair is fine. Come, sit down, and we'll have a nice dinner. I didn't tell you about . . ."

"No, I can't eat now. I can't. My stomach gets like this . . . I'm sorry, Krista. We'll have to leave. I have to lie down. Ed, we're going." She turned to Krista and put a hand on her cheek. "You've done a very nice job here, dear. It's a nice place. I'm sure you'll be very happy."

"But, Mom, I have dinner for you. It turned out really well. Honest. You can't just leave without eating anything."

"I am sorry, dear. But your father doesn't like to drive in the snow. We should go before it ices up. You can call one of your friends and have a nice dinner with better company than us."

She picked up the hat and put it on very carefully. Krista's father tied his shoes without saying a word. He grabbed a last handful of nuts for the road.

"Please don't be like me, dear." Krista's mother held her daughter's hands. "You must eat. And keep well. If you ever need any food or anything, just call me, and I'll run out and get it."

"I have plenty of food, Mom. Some of it's even cooked."

"And don't do anything to jeopardize your job or your chance of being promoted. You must make yourself marketable, Krista. That's the secret in this world. That's what young people today don't understand. Find out what is needed and make yourself into that. That's how to succeed in a career. That's how to succeed with a man. Don't lose your head in that poetry. Do that, and you'll be right back home living with us."

She opened the door and began walking down the stairs.

"You really need to put a light in this stairway, dear."

"I left the bags over there," Krista's father said with a mouthful. "Some things you might need. We'll come again. I can't wait to try your cooking." He kissed her and followed his wife.

Krista went behind them and waved from the porch as the car pulled away. It was still snowing. The wind had picked up, and it felt like ice against her face. She locked the door and slowly walked upstairs.

She shut off the oven and leaned against the counter. "These are the people I know. These are the only people I know." She made a fist and banged it down. Two or three glasses fell over. Her head fell forward, and tears started to drop into the sink. "This is all I know. This is all I know. This is all I know."

The bartender put down the glass of wine and took the money from the counter. She pulled the glass closer and looked at herself in the mirror. The couple next to her had been kissing since she sat down. People behind her were laughing and dancing.

"Happy New Year, Krista," she said out loud. There was nobody else to say it to her.

The second glass of wine tasted better, her brain told her. If she stayed until midnight she would switch to champagne. Perhaps by then she would meet someone. He would buy her a glass.

The drunker the couple beside her became, the louder their show of affection. She turned away as far as she could without staring at the old man on her right. He took a sip and scratched himself.

Occasionally men pushed in close to her, trying to get the bartender's attention. One of them spoke to her. "Sorry," he said as his elbow accidentally grazed her head. She watched as he returned to his table and sat almost in the lap of a long-legged, plunging-neckline-wearing red-haired beauty.

As it approached the hour, the crowd got louder. She would finish her drink and go. Other nights, better nights. Perhaps next year. Krista turned to the mirror one more time, but the reflection seemed to avoid her gaze.

Childhood's End

I fell in love with my second grade teacher. She did not reciprocate. She left teaching after our class went through. It wasn't my fault.

She was too kind and gentle to spend her life teaching history and science to suburban brats, some of whom still peed their pants when called on in class.

I was the shy, skinny, short, pale child who sat in the first desk and knew all the answers. A few of my classmates at this age still didn't know how to write or spell their own names. They now work for the US government.

Was Miss Keyes a good teacher? I don't remember. But she was much more attractive than the Good Sisters of Mercy who taught us the rest of the day. Sister Mary Perpetua repeatedly fell asleep in her chair during the afternoon class. One day two boys pushed her gently into the coat closet, and the rest of us left the room by the back door. The next day there she was, back behind her desk teaching a lesson none of us would remember.

Our school operated like the Soviet Union under Stalin. No opposing viewpoints were tolerated. All signs of inquisitiveness or independent thinking were severely punished. Just obey, pray, think pure thoughts, keep your uniform clean, and never question your leaders. Doubt would weaken the society.

One morning Miss Keyes came up behind me and tickled me, and I felt weak from my stomach to my knees.

The highlight of the school day was recess. The little prisoners were let out into the yard for a few minutes before again putting on the yoke of education.

There was the day we were outside and I saw Chucky Leone with his slingshot.

"How many cans can you hit in a row?" I asked him.

"I don't know. Have any money? I'll bet ya," he said.

"I don't have any money. I just wanna know how many cans you can hit."

"I'm not gonna do it unless ya bet me money."

"I have money," a voice came from behind.

It was Robbie Lester. He was fat, loud, and his father was a lawyer.

"I have money," Robbie said. "I'll bet ya can't hit two in a row."

"Two in a row? Hell, I can hit ten. Ya never seen me, have ya?"

"Who cares? I wanna see ya now."

"Okay. How much?"

"A quarter."

"A quarter? If I hit two you gotta give me fifty cents."

"For fifty cents ya gotta hit somethin' good. How 'bout that squirrel over there?"

"That squirrel in the tree? Yeah, I can hit 'im."

"I wanna see ya hit the squirrel. I'll give ya fifty cents."

By this time most of the kids had gathered around us. Chucky was looking for a good rock. He found one and took aim. Quicker than I thought possible the stone was flying through the air, and the squirrel fell out of the tree. We ran over to see. The animal squirmed on the ground, a big red hole on the side of its body. Chucky was laughing as Robbie Lester handed him the fifty cents. Most of the bigger boys yelled "cool," and they pushed each other to try to get a look at it up close. I didn't eat my lunch that day.

The lunchroom smelled of peanut butter and jelly. The children smelled of the middle-class, republican values branded on them by their parents. It was 1968. Every American had an agenda. Civil rights, Stop the War, Women's Rights, the Rights of the Poor. None of these noble sentiments penetrated the walls of the Holy Rosary Elementary School. The only time we saw the color black, it was on our good sisters' habits and our classmates' shiny shoes.

I remember Miss Keyes wearing purple and green and yellow. Some of the more disrespectful imps called her Miss Easter Egg. But she was prettier than any of the snotty girls in class—though I did like Karen Weaver's red hair. She was quiet, and when spoken to, she would look from side to side and then at the ground. Other kids played jokes on her because they realized she would never fight back. Every St. Patrick's Day, from first grade through eighth, the teacher or nun would force Karen to stand before the class and dance an Irish jig. She smiled and seemed to enjoy it much more than we did. But as she got older, she was as embarrassed as the rest of us. She was gangly, her nose had grown large, and she had lost her freckles.

Back in the second grade, though, it was still cute. Parents, teachers, nuns, all of them love the cute quiet little achiever. They can exploit him, bludgeon the other children with his example, trot him out to show how successful their teaching or parenting methods are. Perhaps that's why the other students pulled pranks on Karen, all freckles and ribbons and shiny hair.

They would hide her belongings, break her pencils, face her desk toward the back of the room. She never cried or did much of anything but look down and stand waiting as if someone would come to protect her.

I felt sorry for her, but what could I do? I was short, small, skinny, scared. It wasn't as if she was Miss Keyes. For her I would have fought the whole Red Army, but she didn't need my assistance. Karen Weaver did.

One day I walked into the classroom and saw Robbie Lester open Karen's desk. He took out all her books and threw them into the trashcan in the back of the room. It was Karen's birthday. She was late because her mother had baked cupcakes for everyone and therefore was giving Karen a ride to school. Lester thought it would be a great joke that, while all the other students would be eating cupcakes, she would open her desk and find everything gone. He warned all of us not to say a word. "I can kill any of you," he said.

Karen's mother walked her into the room. Everyone said, "Hello, Mrs. Weaver." She put the cupcakes on Miss Keyes' desk and kissed Karen on the forehead. The little redhead went to her seat. We all said the Lord's Prayer and then stood for the Pledge of Allegiance. Instead of focusing on the flag in the corner of the room, most eyes were fixed on the treats we soon hoped to eat. I could see the chocolate-iced peaks rising from the box and thanked the Lord for blessing us with mothers who loved to bake.

We sat, and roll was called. That's when Karen decided to open her desk. I sat one row to the right of her. I tried not to turn my head, but I didn't want to miss anything. At first she just stared into the empty space. Names were being called and children yelled out, "Here." Karen was still holding up the top of her desk when Miss Keyes said, "Karen Weaver?" No answer. "Karen Weaver?" Miss Keyes looked up from her book. Karen had put her head inside the empty desk and was crying. None of us had ever seen her show any reaction before. Perhaps she thought her special day would exempt her from the usual treatment. Not even cupcakes could protect her.

When Miss Keyes realized what had happened, she was furious. She took Karen out of the room. None of us knew where. Then she came back and slammed shut the classroom door.

"I want to know right now who did this and why."

I never saw her with such a mean face. She looked like my mother.

"If someone doesn't speak up you'll all be sorry for a long, long time."

I loved Miss Keyes. I did not want to see her upset. Even though I didn't love Karen Weaver, I didn't think it right she should be made to cry. Why should I protect Robbie Lester? Somehow, inside my weak little mind my sense of right and goodness overcame my fear.

"I saw something in the trashcan in the back of the room," I shouted out.

Miss Keyes dumped the trashcan onto the floor, and Karen's books and belongings came tumbling out. A few students helped her gather them up and wipe them off.

"Does anyone know who did this?"

No one answered.

"Joseph, do you know who did this?"

"No." I trembled. "I just saw them in there."

She looked at me sternly. I had never lied to her before. I wanted to run away. That was when I realized I was capable of disappointing someone I loved. I was the one who had been tickled, but now I was just another human being.

Robbie Lester stopped me in the schoolyard on my way home. He pulled on my tie and asked me why I did it, why I told. I didn't say anything.

"What's a matter? Can't talk? You couldn't shut up in class."

He started pushing me.

"You got a big mouth in class but you're just a sissy out here. Aren't ya? Answer me, sissy boy. I told ya not to say anything. You like that little red-haired girl? Huh? You like her? You know, redheads come from the devil."

"You're from the devil!" came out of my mouth.

He stepped forward and slapped me hard. I didn't move. I didn't cry. No one helped me. They were all scared of him. I could hear my heart beating, and it felt as if I was floating away from everyone and stood alone. He must have been saying something, still talking to me. I heard a few words.

"You won't do that again, will ya? . . . all thought it was funny. It was just a joke . . . Do it again and you'll see what happens."

He walked past me and then pushed me from behind. I fell forward on my knees and ripped my pants. Both knees were bleeding. Some of the other kids laughed at me. Right away I started to think of the story I'd have to make up to tell my parents. Another lie.

I did have some friends when I was a young boy. We played games, and on Saturdays we'd follow the creek to the old abandoned factory and look for treasures. All we ever found were little white rubber things that looked like un-blown up balloons. They were always sticky.

All these activities were just ways to mark time until the coming of the most joyous event of the year: summer. A middle-aged man, an old man loses the ability to foresee happiness in his unknown future. Dread and anxiety accompany many of his waking and sleeping hours. But a schoolboy counts off the spring days with wondrous anticipation. The afternoons are warm. Birds are singing through the open classroom windows. Sometimes a bee enters and buzzes around the teacher's head. Our gaze would wander from the blackboard to the blacktop outside. As soon as we were free, ties and jackets would come flying off as we got one day closer to the removal of the yoke.

The nuns struggled to keep our attention.

"You must obey your parents and teachers at all times. The way of the righteous is the way of obedience. It is what the Lord demands of us at all times."

But the way of obedience was a life without joy, a life without laughter and play, a cloistered life. Rigidity. These empty words floated around our heads and flew away on the warm breeze. As the calendar pages turned, there was no holding us back.

Finally June. Each morning I woke up with the sun and watched my favorite cartoons before getting dressed. Mother poured the cream and cereal in the bowl and packed the lunch and fixed my hair and kissed my adorable face and off I went.

Every day the same.

One morning there were no cartoons. A man with glasses was sitting behind a desk. He was talking to another man holding a microphone. Then the picture switched to a long car with a coffin. People in the street were crying. Everyone was wearing black. I asked my father what had happened. He said a man had been shot.

"Who?"

"Robert Kennedy. He was running for president."

"What did he do? Why was he shot?"

"Because he spoke his mind. People don't like that."

My mother wiped away tears as she poured the cereal and packed the lunch and kissed my head. She held onto me extra long before sending me on my way. I didn't understand. A man was killed because of his words. The men I saw on television every night dying in the war carried guns. Their mothers or fathers always got to keep the flags that covered their coffins.

When I reached the schoolyard I saw that our flag was only halfway up the pole. I was on my way to tell one of the sisters when I noticed Robbie Lester in the middle of a crowd of kids. I wondered who he was beating up. I walked over to see and heard they were talking about the man who had been murdered.

"My daddy says our country's in a whole lot of trouble. All the good men are being killed."

"You don't know what you're talkin' about," Lester said.

"My daddy says we should . . ."

"Your daddy's full of shit. I'm glad Kennedy was shot He deserved it. Now Richard Nixon can become president."

The bell rang, and we had to line up. I'm so sorry for my silence.

A Blessing of Silence

The rain fell hard out of the October sky. Mrs. Nielsen could hear it beat down upon the metal awning her husband had erected when people still gave cocktail parties and enjoyed talking to each other with a drink in their hand as they watched the sun set. She no longer went out to the patio. Her granddaughter said weeds were growing in the cracks between the stones.

She was sure the garden must be a mess. There had been so much rain. And the summer was so hot, many days she was too ill to move. It was much easier for Mrs. Nielsen to work inside where everything had assumed its proper place, and there were no surprises. Even the dust and the spiders were not a vexation. She removed them one day, and they returned the next. It was a purposeful life.

Most of her time was spent alone. She was comfortable in her house. If she went to live somewhere else, would they have a chair which fit her perfectly like the one Harry bought for fifty dollars, which reclined just enough so she could put her feet up without blocking the television? She liked the colors, had gotten used to the smells, and tolerated the odd noises of her home. Her daughter said it was like a museum, only no one came to visit. They didn't need to; it was full enough as it was.

Just the other day Mrs. Nielsen had been up in the attic, and she found the paintings Harry had given her when they were married. They were of her. Could she ever truly have been that beautiful? She picked up one with a gold frame and carried it into the bathroom. She held it next to the mirror. What would Harry look like now? Would he have any hair? How could she have changed so much on the outside, become unrecognizable and worn and crinkly, when at times she still felt like the little girl who got lost on the way home from the store and sat down in the street and cried until her mother came and kissed her tears?

A crazy idea entered her brain. She would hang the paintings in the living room, and when the family did visit she would see if they could guess who it was. The only perceptive one was Jill, her granddaughter. The rest of them wouldn't know Charles Darwin from Charles Dickens. She got the stepladder from the closet and put it against the wall. After climbing up, she tried to take down the hideous abstract whatever-it-was the next door neighbor had given her.

There was a knock at the door.

"Nana. Nana, are you home?"

It was Jill.

"Nana, don't be afraid, I'm coming in. I brought you some flowers. Nana! What are you doing?! Don't move. I'll catch you."

"But I'm not falling."

Jill ran to her grandmother and hugged her around the legs.

"I know you're glad to see me, child. But can't you wait 'til I come down?"

"I'm making sure you don't fall."

"Let me go before you cut off the circulation."

"I will if you promise to come down. What if you fall and hit your head and pass out and I have to carry you to your bed or to the hospital and I can't do it because right now I have the wrong shoes on?"

Mrs. Nielsen negotiated the three steps without a problem and turned to face the flustered young woman.

"You might think I'm an invalid the way you fuss after me."

"Nana, you know you shouldn't be up on a ladder. Anything you need done, I can do it. Not right now, because I don't have my work clothes on. Just call me first. You remember when Great Aunt Anabelle fell of that ladder and broke both her hips?"

"Anabelle is a tart who drinks Jack Daniels for breakfast. I'm sober, and I just want to take that awful thing off the wall."

"Nana, come and sit down, and I'll make you some tea. I bought some beautiful flowers at the market. I'll fix them for you. You need flowers in here."

Mrs. Nielsen adjusted the strands of hair that had fallen out of her bun. When was the last time she had worn her hair down?

"I used to have flowers in here all the time," she said as she sat in her favorite chair. "When I could get out in the garden, I would have them all around, in every room."

Jill was already in the kitchen putting the teapot on the burner. After a few minutes she returned with orange and yellow flowers neatly arranged. She put the vase on the windowsill.

"Can you see them from there Nana?"

"Yes, I can see them, dear. They look very nice."

"How are your eyes today, Nana?"

"My eyes are fine, don't you worry. I see. I just see differently than you. I see what has disappeared."

He turned over, tangling the covers and throwing a pillow on the floor. He was not asleep. In the darkness the red numbers on the clock would be clearly visible. Even if he took a quick look his brain, which was constantly concerned with calculations, would start counting the minutes he had left. Each one would slip away, and his head would pound, and the alarm would ring, and he would get no rest at all, and he would be miserable on a day that could be wonderful.

Fluffing the flat pillow, he tried once more. Thinking calmly and breathing deeply, he drifted until he found himself on stage singing and playing guitar. He was good. People were cheering. He knew all the words. It was so effortless. The songs just came to him, inside his head, in his ears, loudly in his left ear. He raised his head. It was the radio alarm.

Moaning, he reached over and slammed the button on top of the clock. It was so early. He was crazy, wasn't he, for even thinking of doing such a thing and getting up hours before he had to? But there was no chance of falling back asleep, and he had to get himself going if he wanted to make it on time.

Cold wooden floor, even with socks on. He felt his way to the window. No. Not possible. It was raining. The little bastard raindrops couldn't even wait until later in the day when it did not matter. How could he do it in the rain? When one conceives the perfect plan, he forgets that no other element in the universe has agreed to cooperate.

The clock said 6:18. He had ten minutes. Not even enough time to shave. Five minutes in the bathroom, five minutes to get dressed. If he got there late it would all have been for nothing. The light in the bathroom was much too bright. His eyes were almost closed as he washed and brushed and peed and gargled. Back into the bedroom to put on the clothes he had laid out, perfectly color—coordinated. Check the money in his wallet, handkerchief and keys. Maybe the rain had stopped. Of course not. No need to comb his hair. Grab the coat and hat. 6:31. He closed the door softly and hurried down the hall.

Old Charlie was coming out of his apartment, but he had no time to chat. As he walked to his car the rain was cold, and it made him sad as rain always did. Then the car wouldn't start so he sat there with his head against the wheel, asking for a life unlike his own.

He opened his eyes, and nothing had changed, so he turned the key once more. The old engine came to life, and before she could change her mind he pulled out onto the road.

His fingers froze as they held the wheel. He had no gloves, and soon he would be shivering. He tried blowing on his hands, but that only made the windshield fog. Through the streaky glass he saw the lights of the store. *Open 24 Hours.* Quickly he found a parking place, hesitated, then shut everything off and ran inside.

"If they don't have them," he thought, "what will I do?"

But there they were, waiting for him. Perfect. As planned. He paid, and shielded them his purchase from the rain as he hurried back to the car. The old girl kicked in right away, and he whispered a thank-you as he patted the dashboard and got back on the road.

He could make it if there wasn't too much traffic. He could make it if all the lights cooperated. He could make it if his feet didn't freeze and fall off. Sitting at a red light he nervously looked at his watch. Seven minutes! Good thing the cops were all at the doughnut shop.

Just a few more blocks. If he could pull this off, it would be something, something to remember. Up ahead he could see the building and the sign that was lit by Christmas lights year round. He was just going to make it. As he turned into the lot he could see her walking to her car.

She had accepted him, taken him into her sweet life, loved him. He had existed in the confinement of his own mind. She was just a noise outside, a distraction, something to be ignored. But somehow she found a way inside with her laughter and fierce eyes. She was about to open her car door.

He left the motor running and approached softly behind her. She heard him, though, and turned, ready to scream. When she saw him she relaxed, but then became confused.

"What are you doing here?"

"I thought I would see you off. See you on your way."

"See me off? It's seven o'clock in the morning. Did you know that?"

"Oh, I know it."

"What have you got behind your back?"

She tried to reach behind him, but he fended off every one of her attempts. The rain had slowed to a fine drizzle, and a few drops could be seen in her hair.

"Do you have something for me?" she asked sweetly.

"Maybe."

"Is it a present?"

"Maybe."

"Oh, you know I have to go." She pretended to be angry. "Why don't you just give it to me?"

She turned her back to him and waited. He kissed her soft wet neck and brought his right arm around in front of her body. It held twelve purple roses.

"Oh, no. Oh my God, you didn't!"

"Happy birthday, Constance Nielsen."

"I don't believe it. You remembered."

She turned to face him and brought the flowers up to her nose.

"They smell so wonderful. Thank you."

"They're not easy to find."

"Someone like you is not easy to find."

She stared at him with those eyes, trying to discern if he was real or just a dream. Her hand went behind his head so she could pull him close and kiss him.

"Don't stop," he said.

"But you know I have to go."

They held each other as the rain came down.

Jill's boot heels made a disturbing thump above Mrs. Nielsen's head.

"What is she doing up in that room? Always some sort of noise. Distracting me . . . How quickly it fades away. Like a tissue, torn apart."

"Nana." Jill was running down the stairs. She was carrying a beat-up old box which she dropped heavily beside Mrs. Nielsen's chair. "Nana, look at what I found up there. There are pictures of you and Grandpa that I've never seen. All these old photos. Look at this baby."

"That one's your mother."

"This is like a treasure chest of stuff. I could go through this all day." Jill suddenly looked up. "Oh, Nana, I'm sorry. If this makes you sad, I'll put it back. I wasn't thinking. I just got so excited when I found everything."

"That's all right, dear. It doesn't make me sad. I'm happy with the life I've lived."

"I guess you wish Grandpa was still here. I miss him. You must miss him."

"Whatever is is what's meant to be. He had his time, and I have mine."

"Are you afraid of dying, Nana?" Jill jumped to her feet. "Oh, forget that. Forget I even asked you that. I don't know what I was thinking. Crazy thoughts just come into my head."

She kissed her grandmother and began to put the photographs back into the box.

"I used to be afraid when I was young. I was afraid of all things. But it turns out being fearful just seems to be a waste of time."

"You're very wise, Nana."

"I'm very old, dear."

"I know you want to rest, Nana. I'm sorry I stayed so long. I just got wrapped up in these things. It's so fascinating to me, all these memories of my family. All these things that happened before I was born. I'll put the box back upstairs and . . ."

"You can take it with you if you want. Nobody's looked at them for years. Just bring it back when you're finished."

"I can? Oh, Nana, that's great. I'll be so careful with them." Jill picked up the box and began to back toward the door. "I don't mean to bother you so much, but I just want to make sure you're all right. You don't mind me checking up on you, do you? Anything you need, I'll come right over. You have my number, right? I can be here in a flash."

"I know, dear."

"So, you'll be all right if I leave now, Nana?"

"I'll be fine."

"Mom sends her love. She'll call you. I love you, Nana. Take care of yourself. And don't climb up any more ladders."

The front door closed, and a few seconds later the screen door slammed. Mrs. Nielsen leaned back, removed her glasses, and shut her eyes.

"That's better. Now I can see everything."

El Perdido

The dog didn't make a sound. The tourists walked past him, wiping their brows and making plans for dinner. The Mexicans stood outside their stores smiling and singing songs. The people on the beach were drinking, their children burying each other in the sand. A man in a droopy hat played guitar, passing between the tables in a bar with no one paying attention.

The dog's black tail never moved, never flinched, not even to scare away the flies. The pigeons paid him no mind, but the strange black birds with long beaks kept their distance. He was a big dog splayed in the center of the square. The midday sun beat down on his body. Dust and stones were kicked up by the feet which always just seemed to miss him.

Still, not a hint of life. No acknowledgement of any existence, even his own. Jack Sloane understood. He had been watching as he sat in the shade. The locals, the tourists, always engaged in meaningless movement. Only the dog and he knew it was useless.

"We're never going to get there. I've never been on a ride like this in my life."

The bus bounced up and down on the uneven Mexican road. Jack and Kathy Sloane held on to the bar above them, trying not to knock into each other.

"Are you sure we're on the right bus? Are you sure we're going the right way? Does it always take this long?"

Jack looked at her but didn't answer.

"That face again. You always give me that face."

"It's the only one I have."

"Years ago you had another face. A nicer one."

He stared out the window until they arrived in town.

The day was hot and uncomfortable. Kathy Sloane walked behind her husband, disgust barely hidden by designer sunglasses.

"I don't like this town at all."

"You just got here."

"It looks like a two-bit town to me. Not like where we are."

"Where we're staying isn't real. You wouldn't even know you were in Mexico."

"That's just the way I like it. Wake up in the morning and look out on the ocean from your own private balcony. Go down to the private beach where a good-looking young man brings you a drink. Later have a snack by the private pool and dip your toes. I would have been such a good queen. Don't you think? Living the royal lifestyle. Wouldn't you like to be my king?"

By the time she had finished her rambling fantasy Jack had stopped listening. There was so much more to interest him—the restaurants, the stores, the people, all crowded into a space that seemed too small, too dense. Yet there was a freshness, an openness. He wanted to hear the language and smell and feel and not have his first impressions tainted by her endless . . .

"I'm really thirsty. Is there any place around here to get something to drink?"

"Look around. There are bars and restaurants everywhere. Why don't you take off those glasses? See where you are. Look outside yourself for a change. You might like it."

"I just want a drink. I don't want a lecture. Can't we just find someplace where I can rest and look at the water?"

"Every one of these places faces the ocean."

"Just pick one. I'm so exhausted after that bus ride I can't even think. What made you want to take that awful bus?"

"The girl at the desk said . . ."

"Oh, God, the girl at the desk again! Please, I don't want to hear any more about the girl at the desk."

They walked in silence. Jack pointed to a place where they might stop. She shrugged her shoulders. He went in. She followed.

The bar was noisy and crowded with Americans showing off their suntanned arms and legs. A man led them to a table and handed them menus. Jack opened his. Kathy stared out the window.

"What are you looking at?"

"Just the ocean. It calms me."

"Great view, isn't it?" A tall, pale gentleman appeared at their table. "I would sit here all day myself just looking at it if I didn't have so much to do."

He pulled up a chair and sat down between them.

"You two just get in?"

"We got here Sunday," Jack answered.

"That's good. Good day to arrive. How long ya stayin'?"

"Until Friday."

"Good. Ya still got a few more days. Where ya from?"

"United States. Philly. You're from Boston, right?"

"Ya got me. Can't hide it. It sticks out like the big nose on my face. But I've been down here twelve years now. Don't regret one minute of it. All that snow and shovelin' they're doin' back home. Don't miss it."

"You don't have much of a tan for being here twelve years."

Jack examined his pasty face. Kathy hadn't turned her head since he sat down.

"I'm Irish. We don't tan much, ya know? Plus I spend most of my time workin', helpin' people out. Helpin' good people like you folks. My name's Mike."

"I'm Jack."

"Nice to meet ya. It's always nice to see people enjoyin' themselves. Cause that's what it's all about, right? Enjoyin' your life. Especially while you're on vacation. If you two can't enjoy yourselves on vacation you should just pack it in, right?"

"I guess so."

"So, how ya likin' Mexico so far? What fun things have ya done? Where ya stayin'?"

"A friend of Kathy's gave us her place for a week."

"Nice. Very nice. Always good to get the freebies, right? Never turn that down. So, you don't own anything yourself?"

"No."

"Well, I can tell from just lookin' at the both of you that you have class." He kept turning his head from one to the other, but Kathy just sipped her drink loudly and looked out the window. "Some people just have that class, that style. They know what they want, and when an opportunity presents itself they go after it, right? As soon as you walked in I felt like I knew ya. How d'ya like this place? The owner's been here now for thirty-two years. Authentic Mexican cuisine. Authentic Mexican sounds and smells, if ya know what I mean. The owner, she's a friend of mine. I help her run the place. Don't do too much, just what I hafta. I'm in Mexico, right? I been here twelve years. Once ya get here ya don't wanna leave, right?"

"I don't know. We just got here."

"When it's time to leave, you won't wanna leave. And when ya get back home, all you'll think about is comin' back. You'll remember all the fun ya had, all the romantic moments.

Moments ya shared together. Moments like right now. You're makin' a memory right now."

Mike smiled with only half his face. The other half never took its eye off Kathy.

"I'm gonna help you two out. I'm gonna help ya make a lot more memories. Because that's what I do. Ever since I got here and realized how beautiful it all was I've dedicated myself to helpin' people enjoy their lives as much as I enjoy mine. Nothin' makes me happier than helpin' people. Because when we get to this point in our lives, what da hell else is there? Right?"

"Sure."

"Let me show ya somethin'. Ya like where you're stayin'?"

"It's nice."

"I can tell you two like to live in style. You go on vacation you like to relax, kick back, a little wine, ocean view, not stuck in a shack with the banshees runnin' around all night, am I right? Well, look at this. This is a map of the Golden Mayan Retreat, an exclusive luxury time share that'll be the best thing to happen to Mexico since Pancho Villa. Wherever it is you're stayin' now I guarantee this has ten times more of everything. Golf courses, tennis courts, private zoo, wildlife safari, private landing strip, casino, five-star restaurants, concert hall, a Catholic church, a mosque, and a synagogue. You can fly right in from the United States and you never have to leave the grounds. Don't even have to worry about speakin' Spanish. Every staff member speaks perfect English. Just like us guys."

"But you can leave if you want?"

"Sure. If ya wanna' Habla some 'spanol with the natives you can get a taxi right at the gate that'll take ya downtown if ya like that sort of thing. They put a red bracelet on your wrist.

"That way we know you're one of ours when ya try to get back in.

"Twenty-four hour security is one of our main features."

"And I guess you want us to go look at a model or something right now."

"Only takes one hour. And then ya get a free lunch, best buffet on the beach. No expense, no pressure, no commitment. Of course, if ya both like it, and frankly I don't see how people like you wouldn't, you can purchase today. Lock up five weeks a year or fifty weeks a year. The more weeks the more memories, right?"

"Sounds good. Leave us some information and we'll . . ."

"I can make you an appointment right now." He pulled out his cell phone and pressed some buttons.

"Well, I don't know. I don't think we're ready to look at anything right now." Although for one splendid moment Jack wondered if he should say yes just to see the look on his wife's face.

"It's not far. They'll even send a car for you."

"Maybe later in the week."

"Whatever you do, I'm your contact. Ya let me know, and I'll set anything up. Like I said, no pressure. We're in Mexico. It's all laid back, all the time. We're not in Boston or Philly, right? No hustle, no bustle, no fuss here. Take your time. Enjoy yourselves. Look around. Get to know us. I say us because it's twelve years now. Every day in paradise. It's a blessing, right? People back home, they don't know. But people like us, we know, right?"

"Sure. Well, we'll think about it."

"That's right. Relax. Think about it. Only don't ya think too hard. You're still on vacation, right? Go with your impulse. Go with your feeling. That's what I always say. Man, it sure was nice talkin' to good people like you. I knew as soon as ya walked in that we'd have a good conversation, a rapport, right? I wasn't wrong about that. I'm never wrong about people. Well, I been wrong about a couple of women. More than a couple. But you don't wanna hear about that. Nah, I'll leave that for the next time we talk. Now you two wait right here. I got somethin' for ya."

Mike pushed back his chair and left them alone. Kathy removed her glasses and turned toward her husband.

"Why do you waste time with people like that? That's thirty minutes of my life that I'll never get back."

"Why not hear what he has to say? He's just trying to make a living. He's not hurting anyone."

"He hurt my ears. He hurt my brain. I came to this country just to sit and relax and look at the ocean. I want no stress. I'm supposed to be de-stressing. Relaxation. Comfort. Calm. Serenity. Everything that's positive. Positive energy. Positive vibes. Do you get it? I don't want someone trying to sell me something I don't want to buy. This is my vacation. It's not even a full vacation. It's only a few days. A few days of peace and quiet. That's all. That's all. Not someone talking my ear off."

"Don't worry. I won't say another word."

She still had a face that would stop a man from thinking about anything else once he saw it, only the slightest hint of lines around the mouth that never seemed to smile anymore. Jack remembered when her dark eyes always looked into his.

"Here he comes again."

"Ya know what? Because you two are such nice people I wanted to give ya somethin'. Come in again, anytime, and ya can buy one martini and get the second free. Our bartender Joe makes the best martinis I've ever had. You'll like 'em, I'm sure. If ya wanna see me, I'm here from two to seven every day. No morning hours in Mexico, right? But the bar's open 'til two a.m. Ya can always leave me a message if I'm not here. If ya decide to see the place, or if ya wanna talk about somethin' else. It's good to talk to people who feel the same way about things, right?" Mike shifted his weight from one leg to the other. He put his hands in his pockets.

"Well, it was great meetin' ya both. I'm sure ya wanna relax and enjoy your drinks. It's a shame ya only have a couple a days left. But if ya wanna do somethin' exictin' I got just the thing. I can set ya up with this great . . ."

"Excuse me, Mike? Is that your name? We just came in here to sit and have a drink. We didn't expect a sales presentation or to be bombarded with information. We don't want to buy anything. We don't want to look at anything. We don't want to ride around from place to place. We don't want to have long conversations. We don't want to get to know the real Mexico. We just want to sit and relax and look at the water. Okay? Is that okay?" Kathy said. "I hope that's okay with you."

"Oh, sure. Sure. Ya go right ahead. Be my guest. There's not a better place in town to enjoy the view than from right here. Like I said, I'd sit and look at it myself if I had the time. But I got some stuff goin' on at the bar right now, people I'm talkin' to. So, if ya need me I'll be right over there. Easy to find. That's why I wear this shirt. So, I'll be goin' over there now."

"Thank you, Mike." Kathy didn't quite smile at him.

"No problem. No problem."

Mike moved away quickly, and they sat in silence.

"You amaze me," Jack finally said.

"What?"

"Why are you so rude? Why would you speak to someone like that? The man's just doing his job. Just like you try to do your job back home. In fact, he's very much like you. Your jobs are similar."

"He's nothing like me!" Kathy sat straight up and laughed. "We have nothing in common. I'm a professional, certified, with years of training. He's some bozo in a Hawaiian shirt who hangs at a bar."

"When did you become so cruel?"

"Cruel? I'm the most thoughtful person you'll ever meet."

"I'm so fucked."

"And why do they have to keep playing that stupid music?"

A mariachi band had entered the bar. They stood in the back playing what they thought the tourists wanted to hear.

"They're good. They're the best I've heard so far."

"Everywhere we go people are playing music and asking for money. Even on the bus. You can't get away from them. Why can't they just stay at home? Why do they have to keep following us?"

"While you were waiting for your bags at the airport, I paid a special fee so that we'd have music wherever we went."

Kathy was not amused.

"You think you're so funny," she sneered. "Always with a joke. Especially with that stupid little girl who works at the front desk. What's her name?"

"Iveth."

"Iveth? What kind of name is that? And you knew it right away, didn't you? You didn't hesitate. You're in love with Iveth. I saw you smiling at her, talking to her every chance you get. Why don't you just marry her and be done with it?"

"She's not even twenty years old."

"Well, you can wait a couple of years. You've got a couple of good years left. You can come back here, see Mike and buy a time share, ask Iveth to marry you, and you two can live together in Mexico and be happy and listen to this stupid music every day of your lives."

"She has a sweetness about her, and at least she smiles."

"Well, I guess she has something to smile about."

Jack sighed. "Why can't you be a bit positive, just once?"

"Positive? How can I be positive when all this negative shit keeps raining down on my head? Nothing good ever happens. Every time I look forward to something, it turns out to be nothing. Every time I have a good feeling, it's crushed. Do you know what it's like to be disappointed every day of your life? I go to sleep and I have beautiful dreams and then I wake up to my life again. Nothing has ever worked out the way I wanted. Nothing! What kind of life is that? I pray, I try to be good, treat people the right way, do everything the right way, and what do I get? This life. My life. I don't understand it. I don't understand what went wrong. Why has it ended up like this?

Why can't I be happy? Everything's so heavy. My head feels so heavy. I'm tired of carrying it around. I'm tired of everything. I thought I could come down here and relax and shut my brain and not think for a few days. Just a little break. A break from the thinking. That's the worst part. My brain never shuts off. Always working, working, working. It's like a disease. How do you stop it? How can you make it stop? Do you know? If you know, I wish you would tell me. I wish you could tell me something that would make me laugh again. Or smile. But I've already heard everything you have to say."

Kathy sipped the last of her drink and adjusted her hat.

"La cuenta, por favor."

The waiter brought the check and Jack paid. Mike waved, and the waiter grinned as he got up from the table. *"Gracias, señor.* Come back." His wife was already waiting outside.

"Which way do we go?" Kathy asked.

"I know the way."

They walked.

"Are you sure you know where you're going?"

"I'm sure."

"Do you want to ask someone?"

"No."

The sun was low in the sky. She trailed behind.

"Are you sure you know where you're going? I don't remember any of this."

"I don't need you to remember it. I remember it."

"I don't think you know where you're going. Why don't we ask someone?"

"It's not necessary."

"I still think it's a good idea. You may not remember so well after that beer you had."

"You go ahead and ask. I'll keep going."

"You would leave me, wouldn't you?'

"Just follow me, and you'll get where you want to go."

"That hasn't worked for twenty years. Why should it work now?"

Jack didn't even have the strength to shake his head.

"I'm never coming back here again," she said.

Constant noise. There was no relief. His hands were tied behind his back. His head was throbbing in the dark. He heard a language he didn't understand, and then a light flashed before his eyes. He felt the heat. His sweat was dripping. Why had they brought him to this place? Someone held the torch close to his head. His eyes burned, and his head. That pounding. Pounding. Whispered words and what sounded like laughter. They were looking him over. He realized he was naked, on view for these people with strange markings on their faces. He could see them now as they each lit a torch and stood in a circle around him. They didn't touch him. Strangely, he felt no fear. One of them made a sound like a bird. He was answered by another in the dark distance. The air was filled with these eerie, haunting cries. Then, one by one, the strangers started to move. One of them nudged him gently forward, and he followed. His feet were bare but nothing pricked them, as if a carpet of flowers had been laid in his path. They walked slowly through the forest. He wanted to speak to them, to find out why. Then, suddenly, he was standing alone on the stage of an outdoor theater. Rows and rows of people were staring at him. They were dressed in robes of different colors. No one made a sound. They were waiting for him to act, to move, to do something. He was also waiting. He had been waiting his entire life.

"Come," said the voice behind him. He turned to see a series of steps leading up to the sky. "Come, your wait is over." Her words tumbled like a waterfall into his thirsty ears. The stairs were covered in mist, and his steps were unsteady. But the kind ones who had guided him through the forest reappeared with their torches to light his way. He ascended slowly, looking at each of their faces. Then he realized what that pounding was in his brain. The higher he went, the louder the drums became. But now they were soothing, rhythmic, calling him forward. He began to tire until he heard the most beautiful song. A melody of love and compassion, it pulled him upward. He was floating above the steps until again he was alone. He had been tricked. Misled. Nothing had changed. He began to shiver.

"Do not fear. Do not fear ever again." She was standing before him, covered in a robe of red and gold. She wore silver bracelets, and her black hair was long. Her eyes showed kindness. She was surrounded by many attendants. Two of them came forward and began to rub his body with oils. They laid flower petals on the ground between them. The drums beat, and the moon and stars appeared in the sky. Women began to sing, and men began to dance. Her dark eyes never left his. Two girls removed her robe as she came forward to embrace him. Around them swirled a whirlwind of sound and light. They began to make love. The people in the audience stood and applauded. Some tried to climb the steps. He tried to protect her, lock her in his embrace forever. They were pulling at her, screaming for her. Tearing her away. He tried to hold on. One more kiss. Look into her eyes again. They were on every side of her. He flailed at them. It was no use. She was fading, and all he saw was their faces. Those same faces. Every day of his life.

Jack raised his glass and took a long, slow drink. The beach was full of tourists trying to live a dream and locals trying to sell them one. Fishermen dropped their lines off the pier while the pelicans waited for the ones they threw back. The smell of the sea mixed with suntan oil and the ever-present tacos was making him sick. He read the sign again and it made him laugh. Playa de los Muertos.

He left the bar and walked along the beach. The sky over the ocean was getting darker. Wind blew sand down the back of his shirt. He turned away from the sea. The streets of the town went straight up into the mountains. Jack thought of other trips he had taken when he was younger, walking down unknown roads, hoping to meet, hoping to find something. Chance, a promise, a possibility. If a lovely girl went into a shop or a restaurant, he would follow. *She takes off her sunglasses and looks just once . . .*

Lazy drops of rain began to fall. The sky overhead was black. The bikini-clad women and pot-bellied men ran for cover. Jack continued to walk. As he passed one establishment after another, occasionally someone would call out to him. "*Señor,* come inside. We have beer." His boots sank into the wet sand. Kathy was back there, waiting for him. "They told me it never rains here," she had said. Nothing had been as promised. He still had not seen one iguana.

Face to Face

Civilization continued its progress outside his locked windows. It was the symphony of business as usual: slamming car doors, revving engines, hammering workers, shouting bosses.

Business was good. Increased noise meant increased productivity, everything growing and flowing. Constant movement and struggle. The advancement of the people.

John Bishop rose wearily and covered his ears.

"Goddamned industrial wasteland."

As a young man he had been drawn to a higher calling. He knew he was marked, ordained for a life beyond. He would be chosen for a sacred mission. Have visions, hear voices. An ordinary life would not be possible.

"All those people out there. There's enough of them to do everything the world needs them to do. Have babies, wear uniforms and wave flags, make things and sell things. And every one of them believes they're living a life of importance."

He knew better.

He had waited for the summons, the idea, the breath of genius. Everyone looked to young John, dashing John, destined for greatness. "Lead us, John. Use us, guide us," their eyes said.

But here he was, scratching himself as he walked to the bathroom. The light he once thought he saw had become so dim even a moth would not be attracted.

It was a small house on a busy highway. The windows were always shut. The downstairs curtains were drawn tight. He only opened the door for himself to pass through.

"How can these people live like this? They're not anyone I would ever want for my friends, they're only obstacles I have to overcome. Rudeness, stupidity, and endless, useless conversations. They only exist to make noise and ruin my peace of mind."

Peace of mind. He laughed. In this place?

Before he knew the world there was a time when he would sit and ask questions and listen. That time had passed. There was no revelation, no angel, no burning bush. Prayer had become a ritual, and grace was just somebody's name. All those years of supplication and what had he received? An emptiness that broke his heart.

He looked at the clock. Thirty minutes to get ready. The first blind date of his life. If redemption could not be found within, perhaps someone else could breathe life into his soul—or at least offer a diversion.

John Bishop had been a long time without love. One of the nights he couldn't sleep he spent the dark hours counting how many days it had been. More than three thousand days. Occasionally during a dream he would feel a warm embrace but then wake to find one more day without compassion.

Perhaps the woman he was meeting would change all that.

"We could leave this hellhole. I would never see these people or this place again. We would live in peace and quiet. A place of beauty. Just the sounds of nature. To be able to get away. Just to get away. Is it asking too much for just this one blessing?"

He had to hurry. Shave, wash, dress with clean underwear, comb his hair. He put on his shoes, the ones that made him look taller. A little spray of that scent that drives women wild. He looked in the mirror.

"You are one good-looking man, John Bishop. If I say so myself. There's no one out there at my age that looks this good. At least that's one thing I've kept. All those women who've said no to me, they must be idiots."

One final brush of the hair. A peek out the window, to make sure none of his neighbors were around. He didn't want to see anyone, answer their questions, pretend to smile.

The coast was clear. He locked the door and walked down the driveway.

There were no clouds in the sky. The sun was shining, and creatures were about, birds looking for worms, squirrels hunting for nuts, and the two dogs in the neighbor's yard sitting with their legs wide open licking themselves.

To be so shameless. To live by instinct. That's the mindset John Bishop would adopt. Live like the animal. Love like the animal. See a woman, tell her you want her and take her. That's how he would approach the meeting with—

He had forgotten her name.

"Perhaps she'll be wearing a name tag. No, it's not like one of those meetings for 'Singles Without Hope.' She said she would be the one at the bar with blonde hair and a smile on her face. There can't be more than one woman like that, right?"

John Bishop walked quickly through his neighborhood. His neighborhood. He laughed. He barely knew anyone. Sometimes a nod, occasionally one of them would crack a smile. He knew the dogs better than he knew the people. The dogs greeted him warmly; their owners were busy keeping busy, mowing the lawn or blowing the snow, hammering, drilling, sucking up leaves. What would the town have been like before the motorized hum? A peaceful breeze through the trees. Everyone saying hello and baking pies for each other on Sundays. Smiling and waving and doors wide open. He was born too late to enjoy suburbia.

In the garden outside the Art Center the newly commissioned bronze sculptures were finally in place. The township council had debated for months, seeking the proper spot to display the fine new works. But what were they? Abstract blobs? Inarticulate longings? Representations of an unknowable future?

"Another good place for the birds to sit and poop."

As he turned his head he saw the woman who never spoke to anyone. "Sour Samantha," he called her. In five years he had passed her on the street perhaps one thousand times without ever hearing even a grunt. He imagined she had lost her husband in the war. Or had taken a vow of silence. John remembered something he had read. The writer said the sound of Heaven would be "Music and Silence." Unfriendliness was her way of bringing about paradise.

The walking man flashed, and he stepped off the curb. A car turned the corner and accelerated across his path, just missing him. John Bishop cursed Henry Ford and continued crossing.

He knew he looked good, but what about his breath? He just had time to stop in the convenience store and pick up a packet of the mints that make people smile and dance.

He held the door for two young women as they entered. The second one smelled like vanilla. He brushed back his hair as he followed them down an aisle. What was she wearing? What was the name of those mints? He grabbed a roll of something and stepped up to the counter.

"I'm sorry. I'm closed. You'll have to get in the other line," a pock-faced, mop-haired lad said as he slammed down a "Proceed to Next Line" sign and turned his back. John Bishop ignored his ego, bit his lip, and moved over a few steps behind an older woman purchasing milk. As she counted out her pennies, other customers came and stood behind him. The line grew longer. The woman dug deep into her purse. The teenager who had rejected John was still behind the counter, slowly putting away one pack of cigarettes at a time. He must have heard the murmuring and grumbling because he looked up, shuffled to the register, picked up the sign, and said, "I can help the next customer." People behind him jumped to the other line before John had a chance to move. The woman was now attempting to charge her purchase but she didn't have ID. He reluctantly slid over to the other line but as he approached the counter down came the sign again.

"Are you open?"

"No, sir. You'll have to go to the other line."

"I've been in the other line. Now I'm in this line."

"I can't help you, sir. You can go to the other line."

"Why can't you help me?"

"I'm really just here to stock. I'm not supposed to be ringing."

"Then why are you behind the counter?"

"I'm just backup."

"Backup to what?"

"The primary ringer."

"Then why did you open this line just now?"

"Because we went over the optimum number of customers."

"And that's the only time you can ring?"

"Yes, sir."

"And you can't just take my fifty cents for this pack of mints?"

"Not unless we go over the optimum number of customers."

"It will take thirty seconds."

"Why don't you go to the primary ringer, sir? She's open."

"Because you're standing right here. Just take my money."

"I can't. I'm being watched."

"By God, I hope."

"No, by my manager. He's grading my performance."

"And you want to do well, don't you?"

"Yes, sir."

"You want to keep this job, don't you?"

"Yes, sir."

"Then ring up my goddamned mints! I've been in this store now for fifteen minutes, and I'm still holding this roll of mints in my hand. This is supposed to be a convenience store, for the convenience of the customers and not the employees. People want to get in and get out. We have lives. We don't give a shit about your optimum whatever. You have a service job, son. Service! Do you know what that word means? You serve the customer. Whatever the customer needs, you serve them. You help them. You take care of them. Do you think I or anyone else has time to stand around while you move like Grandma Moses and ignore people? I have a life. Unlike you, you crater-faced imbecile. I want service now! And if you don't ring me up I'll take that sign of yours and shove it swiftly up your ass. Show that to your manager."

John Bishop was so disturbed leaving the store he couldn't open the package, fumbling with it until he threw it to the pavement. Mints flew up in the air as he walked on. Everywhere he turned, surrounded by idiots, closing in on him.

It was unbearable. Where was the one person, the one voice of kindness he always expected to hear? Sweet words were whispered to others, never to him. Even when he was in the mood to greet someone, they simply turned away. Perhaps this woman, the one he was to meet, she would show him the kindness he deserved. What's-her-name.

He turned the corner and wove his way through the couples holding hands. Why did they have to stand outside the restaurant and pose, showing off their togetherness? He opened the door, and a woman walked right through, stepping on his foot with her man-sized shoes without saying a word. He limped inside, giving his eyes a minute to adjust to the darkness.

"Can I help you?"

A young blonde woman in a tight black dress approached John Bishop as he recovered his sight just in time.

"Why, yes. I'm supposed to meet someone here."

'Do you have a reservation for dinner?"

"I believe so. But we're meeting at the bar first."

"Well, if you don't have a reservation for dinner by now, I won't be able to give you one. We're completely booked until 11:00 p.m."

"I'm happy for you. But I believe we have a reservation."

"That's fine. That's good. Why don't I just check on that for you, okay? Then neither of us will have to worry."

"I'm not really worried. There are plenty of restaurants on this street. Good ones. The name is Bishop."

"But not like this one," the myopic hostess said as she squinted at her book. "None of them can do what we do. We're blessed with the best chef in the area."

"Lucky for you, that you work in such a place."

"Yes, I am lucky. And so are you. There is a reservation under Bishop for two." She smiled at him, now that he was in.

"How fortunate."

"When you do sit down and order, you might want to try one of our fabulous steaks. We serve the finest Angus beef in the region. All the customers I've talked to have been extremely pleased with the experience."

"How do the cows feel about it?"

"The cows?"

"Yes, the cows who are slaughtered so you can serve your overpriced meals to 'patrons' who wouldn't know the difference between Angus beef and Dog Chow on a stick."

"I'll have you know, sir, that we serve the finest clientele in the area."

"And you have the finest chef in the area. And the finest servers. And the finest bartenders. And, of course, the finest hostess. I can't tell you how privileged I feel just to be inside this establishment. I'll tell you what, if I have to take a shit,

I won't let my ass touch the toilet. Okay? Call me when my table's ready. I'll be at the bar."

John Bishop walked a slow circle around the bar in the middle of the room. He stared into the face of every woman sitting on a stool. Not one seemed interested in him. Almost every female in the room was blonde. Which one was his? He couldn't even scream out her name. Mabel? Martha? Maribel? Marigold?

"John?"

"Huh?"

"Are you John?"

"Yes."

"Hi. I'm Shelly."

"Oh, Shelly, right. How are you? How do you do?"

Like the gentleman he was, he shook her hand and kept his eyes at face level.

"I'm so sorry I'm late. I got held up at work. There's always so much to do. I get so worried that I'll never catch up. But you can only do so much. You can only do what you can do, right? You can't do more than that. It doesn't do any good to worry about it. I know."

She seemed nervous. As she talked John's gaze began its descent.

"So, have you been here long?" Shelly asked. She didn't give him time to answer. "It's a nice place. But it gets really crowded. I wasn't sure if we should meet here or someplace else, someplace quieter. The food's good here, but it's loud. Next door is quiet, but the food's not so good. Down the street I know a place, we could go there . . ."

"This is fine."

They stood, he with his hands in his pockets and she fixing her hair.

"Do you want a drink? We could get a drink."

Behind them a man with greased hair was yelling into a cell phone. In front of them a husband and wife were arguing about whose turn it was to de-flea the dog.

"Why don't we go to our table?" John suggested. "It will be easier to talk."

"Yes. There's so much to talk about when you meet someone for the first time. Where are you from? What do you do? What do you like? It's exciting, isn't it? All these questions. I don't expect you to answer them all at one time."

"Of course not."

They approached the hostess stand.

"Is our table ready?" John smiled.

Without looking up the young blonde said, "Follow me."

She sat them in a corner and handed them menus. Before she could walk away John asked in a sweet voice, "What do you recommend?"

"That you get stuffed!"

John Bishop laughed so loudly the sous chef came out of the kitchen to see what he was missing.

"People can be so rude," Shelly shook her head. "I feel there's never any reason to be rude. We're all here, we're all human, working toward the same goal. I'm not better than you.

"We all have souls. We all have hearts. We're all just trying to make a connection. Treat people the right way. All the time. Don't you agree? I was reading this book about babies who never got the love they needed. When they were young they didn't have the connection to their mother. It's so important that parents establish that connection with their children. That's why we have so many people who can't relate, who can't love. It's called separation syndrome. They can't connect. They feel separated from everyone. They have all this anger that builds up inside them. And then they just let it loose on everyone they meet. I'm sure you've met a few people who are like that."

John was studying the wine list.

Without looking up he said, "Can't say that I have."

"It's all about that connection. Between parents and children. Between people and people. Adults, I mean. Don't you agree?"

Shelly didn't wait for a response. "What do we have if we can't connect with each other? A lonely world where no one knows anyone, no one sees, no one hears, no one cares. I try to establish that connection with everyone I meet. Even if it's just to say hello, or smile or wave. I know people say, 'Oh, there goes that crazy lady. She's always smiling. She's always happy.' I have a range of emotions just like everyone else. But I try to reach out, be light, be funny. People ask me why I've never been married. I don't know. I'm kind. I'm thoughtful. I know I'm not the best looking woman. But I have a good heart. What do you think?" There was a pause.

John realized he had to say something.

"Would you like something else to drink?"

"Oh, I like wine. But I can't drink too much, because then I never shut up. You're probably thinking, 'She really talks a lot now.' But you should see me with a couple of glasses down the hatch. But I just like people. I like to talk to interesting people. How else will we get to know each other?"

John Bishop ordered one glass of wine for himself.

"It's a nice place, isn't it?" Shelly looked around. "I picked it because every time I come here, people always seem happy. I like being around happy people. It makes me feel like there's a chance for the world. I saw on the news today about that girl who was killed. It's so awful. Killed by her boyfriend. The one she loved and trusted. In her own bed. Awful."

"I don't think we should talk about that at dinner."

"Oh, I know. I know. I don't fixate on tragedy. Some people do, you know. But that's why we have to connect with our children. I'm not a mother. I'm fifty-four. That blessing has probably passed me by. But the mother has to establish a connection with her baby. She has to hold that baby, and that baby has to feel that he or she is loved. That baby has to feel it. Every day. Do you see? Because if that connection is not established, that baby, when he grows up, will never know how to love. And that's why we have murders and beatings and rapes and war. We're separated, but we don't even know it. It happened at birth."

The waitress, another nubile blonde clothed in black, was eager to take their orders.

"I don't want to eat heavy," Shelly said. "I like salads. I like all the different things they put in a salad. That's what I'll have."

"What kind of salad?" the waitress asked ever so politely.

"One with lots of different vegetation. And some fruit."

"We have our Signature Classic. It's the Chef's Special."

"That sounds good. I'd like that."

"I'll also have the Chef's Special Salad. And the Chef's Special Steak." John smiled up at the server. "Then my meal can't be anything but special, right?"

"I'll make sure that it is, sir. That's what we specialize in here, special experiences."

"I feel special already."

She took the menus, and John watched her walk away from the table. Special, indeed.

"I don't get to eat out much. I don't date much, either. We're very busy at work. And then when I get home I'm just so tired. That's why I try to walk, take a little walk around the neighborhood every night. You've probably seen me, boppin' along to the tunes. I wear my headphones. I sing to myself sometimes. Especially if its one of those good old songs, I sing out loud. I love those old tunes, don't you? I don't know if I've seen you around. If I have and I didn't say hello, it's not because I'm ignoring you. I'm so into my music. I would never ignore or be rude to anyone. I even like to say hello to the trees. There are certain beautiful ones I see all the time. I give them names.

"We're all a part of nature. A small little stink bug, a little ant is just as important as I am. Don't you feel that way? That we're all just a small part of something bigger, something huge, something unexplainable. It's something we can't even imagine."

"I certainly can't imagine it." His mouth was watering as he smelled the steaks being served to other tables.

"Within this huge universe we all have our little part. And we all have little moments. That's why I love music so much. I put on the radio and then suddenly one of those great songs comes on. I sing, I dance. It's like three or four minutes of bliss in a world of heartbreak and pain. Then the moment's gone. But there'll be others. You just don't know when. That's what's so incredible. They catch you, and then you want to share it with the whole world."

Shelly had a sweet smile, and John Bishop was just beginning to notice. Her monologue had made him forget the events of the day. He wondered if she was intrigued by his new beard. He continually rubbed his thumb and forefinger slowly against his chin. He liked the feel of it, the smoothness; he liked the way it made him look.

"You're a nice guy. I can tell. You've been listening to me, and I haven't even given you a chance to talk. There's so much I want to say. Most people are like that, right? We just want to connect." Shelly's hands never stopped moving as she spoke. "We want people to know who we are. Why we should be noticed. Why someone should want to be with us and love us. I'm here with you. And I want you to know everything. We should be open. We should be open to the people we meet and to life. I'm fifty-four and I'm not married. I ask myself, 'Why am I not married? Why hasn't that happened for me? Is it because I'm not worth it?' I've seen the way men look at me, or don't look at me. I'm more invisible than Claude Rains. But I keep smiling. I've cried many nights alone. But every day I wake up, and it's a new day. And that could be the day. It only takes one day, one spark, one chance. We have to have hope, right? It's never too late, right?"

"Speaking of late, where is our food?" He gripped his fork impatiently.

"Do you know what some man told me the other day? It's too late for me to get married. He said I should concentrate on doing work for charity, that I should make myself useful. That's what he said. I just smiled. I always smile. I don't get offended. I take it into my heart and offer it up. I know who I am. I know I have a problem with love. Trusting someone, wow. That's hard, right? It's never easy, when you're afraid. When you're afraid that person might just go away. When you get to the point where you convince yourself they'll always be there and then they go away. When you count on them and you expect to see them, call them up, touch them, see them smile. I was too young to realize. Love doesn't keep a person safe. It doesn't matter. Maybe that's why I'm not married. When Jamie died, I lost connection with everything. I had just seen him the day before, and he was happy. I saw him every day. The next day would be the same. He called his father and asked for a ride but his father couldn't make it and told him he'd see him later. Who knows when the time will come when we feel we need help? He had people all around, why was he so alone? Why didn't he call me? He called me every day. Why didn't he call me that day? Can you be surrounded and loved and cared for and still feel close to no one? They didn't even let me see him when I found out. He must have felt empty, loveless, to do such a thing. Loveless. Is there a more horrible word in the English language? Loving no one. Not being loved. He killed me, too. He killed my heart. I was only nineteen. I just froze. I shut it all off. That's when I first saw myself as separate, as moving through space away from everyone else. Oh, I've had years of therapy and I'm definitely better now. I'm better. I can talk to people and smile. You see how I'm talking to you. We're conversing, laughing, smiling, happy. I'm here on a date with you. Trying to connect. Trying to reach out. I can let some people touch me now. It's all positive. I'm moving past it all. The past doesn't affect me. It has nothing to do with me. So long ago. Years ago. I don't think of it. You saw me trying. I was engaged. I was lively . . . One person's not here anymore. Look at all the people who still are here. Good people. People I like to see. People who say hello to me when I walk. But I walk solo. Alone. I always walk alone. People pass by, but no one joins me. People are polite, but no one wants to know me. They see my face and body, and they make their decision. But I have a heart to share. It's real. Why can't I touch someone? Why can't I love? I'm free of it. I'm free from all of it. Memories don't affect me. Memories do not exist. Figments. Figments." Shelly wiped her eyes with one hand and waved the other in the air. "Be gone. Ghosts. Spirits. I'm done with you. What are you to me? I'm in the land of the living. I'm here with—oh, I'm so sorry. I forgot your name."

"It's John."

"That's right, John. That's a solid name. That's a good name. What a nice dinner we're having, aren't we, John? I was talking so much I didn't even notice she brought my salad. My mouth gets so dry sometimes. Does that happen to you? Maybe I should have had that wine. It would relax me. But that's okay, I feel relaxed with you. And I'm not just saying that. Excuse me." She took a long, noisy drink of water. "Yum. That's good water. We have good water in our county, don't you think? Must be purified, right? Take out all the imperfections. That's what we have to do with our minds. Take out all the impurities. Our mind should be just like the water. Calm and pure, right?"

"Right now my mind is very tired. It's been a long day."

"Oh, right. Of course. I understand. I know what that's like. We're all workin' so hard. Workin' hard all the time. Sometimes I think we're just like animals on remote control. One day to the next. One day to the next. Push. Push. Push. Go. Go. Go. We all have our responsibilities. Don't I know it."

The waitress brought the check without asking if they wanted dessert.

"You didn't eat much of your salad."

"Oh, I don't eat much, John. I probably should eat more. But, you know, you have to stay fit. Fit body, fit mind."

Shelly fumbled through her purse, took out her wallet, and began to count the money she remembered to bring.

"Oh, no. Put that away. I'm paying for this," John Bishop said as he stroked his beard. "I enjoyed your company."

"Really?" Shelly lightly touched his arm. "I didn't talk too much? I didn't want to bore you. I just wanted you to get to know me. You really are a nice man. I can tell, even though you didn't talk about yourself much. We could get to know each other more as time goes on."

"Yes."

"It's nice how a relationship can work out. Each person gets to know a little more about the other every time they meet, every time they talk. Each time it gets deeper and deeper."

"Yes, that's nice. Well, I can walk you home if you want."

"Oh, no. Don't worry about that." Shelly again brushed his arm. He held the door for her as they exited the restaurant. "I live right up the street. That's why it's easy for me to get here and to meet you, I mean if we come here again, if we eat again. Of course, we'll eat again. I mean if you want to eat with me, I can get here easily and meet you. If you want to."

"Yes. I'll call you. I have your number."

"You do have my number. You have the right number, because you already called, or else I wouldn't be here. So, do call me."

"Yes, I will. You take care of yourself."

"You, too. Okay. Right. Take care. See ya." She waved. "Bye. Be safe. See ya soon."

The summer sun had not yet set as Shelly walked home. She passed many people, some hand in hand, and she smiled at them all. As she turned into her driveway, she stopped abruptly and brought her hands to her lips. There in the yard was the bunny she had seen out her window every morning. She crept closer, but the animal did not run. Two more steps and she saw why.

Underneath the fur of the mother rabbit were fuzzy babies fighting for food. Squiggling, sucking, trying to keep warm.

She knew he would never call her. Shelly sat on the grass and started to cry.

A Bed of Compassion

"Anna, where are my shoes and socks? Why do you keep moving them?"

He pushed his glasses up on his nose in the hope that they would help him discover her mysterious hiding place.

"Always you're misplacing them. Misplacing everything. And blaming me. When you get to Heaven you'll have no trouble finding your shoes and socks."

"When I get to Heaven I won't have any feet, so it won't matter."

It was much more difficult to do everything now: to walk, to get dressed, even to think. The least she could do is stop hiding parts of his wardrobe.

"You might think you would help me, Anna, knowing how special today is for me."

"What, are you receiving the Medal of Honor or something? Maybe the Nobel Prize?"

"Never mind," he said as he pulled one sock out from under the bed. "What matters to me doesn't seem to matter to you anymore."

Edward Steele now had one sock and one shoe on, and the other foot was freezing.

"You're always blaming me, accusing me of what I don't do," Anna said as she checked on the chicken in the oven. "Who's taken care of you all these years? When you were sick? When you couldn't move around? Who else would have stayed with you all this time?"

"Maybe it's you who are looking for the medal. I'll submit your name to the committee. But if you win I'll have to hear how you have nothing to wear and how you're too fat to fit into anything, and I'd just as soon go crawl into a hole in the garden and be covered up."

"That could be arranged."

Edward found a different colored sock on top of the dresser. He put it on just to keep his foot warm.

"Anna, do you think there is a God?"

The chicken was still half frozen. "You're asking me now? Don't you think it's a little late for that?"

"I'm serious. Do you think there's a God in Heaven, and He's judging us, and keeping track of what we do, and deciding where to send us when we die?"

"I hope He sends me to a place where I don't have to cook for anyone."

"You never take me seriously anymore." Edward was sitting on the bed when she entered the room.

"Why aren't you getting ready? You have to leave soon."

He didn't move. "Does it really matter? Does it really matter if I go or not? If I'm going to Heaven or Hell, don't you think it's already been decided, and maybe I could just sit here and wait for it to happen?"

He was bent over, his eyes looking down at the floor. She could see the top of his head, which she used to love to kiss.

"Come on. It's no good to be thinking like this."

"But don't you think about it? It's going to happen soon."

"What's going to happen?"

"We'll be going. We'll be going wherever we're supposed to go. It could be today or tomorrow. I can't stop thinking about it. Where will I be? Where will you be? Will we be together? If I'm already destined to go to one place, do I have enough time to change His mind?"

"Why don't you write Him a letter?"

"There you go again." He pushed her hand away in disgust. "You have no feeling for me at all. Everything I say is a joke. I stumble around. I can't move right. I can't think right. I'm ready to go. I'm ready to go wherever I'm going. There's no use for me here anymore. No one else needs me. You don't need me. What is the point of living like this? If there's a place for me somewhere I'm ready to see it. Maybe there'll be love and good things there. Maybe I'll be young again. Maybe I'll know, learn something, and I won't be so stupid. At least it won't be this."

"Is it so bad?" Anna asked him gently.

"Knowing it's the end. It scares me. There'll be nothing left of me, nothing left of you."

"So, maybe we can just enjoy what we have."

She held his hand for the first time in years. He was tired, and she helped him back into bed. She lay down beside him, wearily closed her eyes and was soon asleep.

When she awoke her husband was snoring. Anna sat up and stared at the body next to her. His hair was white, his legs were skinny, and his hands and arms were covered with small brown marks. She felt a separation, a withdrawal from who he had become. But wasn't that only a function of her mind? Were they only separate because she thought it to be so? Didn't she still love him? Wouldn't their love be the bond, the link that would carry them together into whatever came next? If she listened more with her heart instead of her torn and frayed ego, maybe it wouldn't be so bad.

"I'll check on the chicken, Ed. You sleep for awhile."

She got up and went into the kitchen. Dinner was almost ready. As she set the table she looked over at the clock.

"He usually watches the news now. He'll miss it." Anna thought about waking him up. But she enjoyed the quiet. There was something she was trying to hear.

One More Day

The planes have been flying over all morning. All night, too. How can I concentrate? I am so tired. Look what it is doing to my face. There is another line. I counted them all yesterday. This is definitely a new one. It is the world that is making me ugly. If I were blessed enough to live in a place of peace and quiet, I would not be aging as I am. I cannot bear to look.

That's not even the worst of it. There was another catastrophe this morning. The old bookshelf fell apart again. Books and papers and magazines everywhere. I just went to pull out one volume. The frame holding the photograph of my father is ruined. It crashed to the floor, and I was picking up pieces of glass for an hour. I can't be doing this. I don't have idle hours like all the other people I see every day.

My time is precious to me. No meaningless chores or wasteful motions. No useless, inane conversations. All hours must be focused to preserve what is essential. I will keep her alive. Nothing will prevent me. Every minute must be used wisely. Of course I will take breaks for meals, and possibly the newspaper.

I dreamt of her again last night. Those are the most wonderful days, when another image of her fills every second. I know it was her because I felt it so strongly. I was walking, and I turned a corner, and there she was! She didn't seem surprised. She expected me. We walked for a while, and then she said something incredible. "Sometimes it's so difficult to tell someone how you feel about them," she said. "How do you feel?" I said. She stopped, and I wanted to put my arms around her, like the first time. But I didn't move. I waited. Finally she said, "We have plenty of time."

I awoke in such a hopeful mood. But these noises. Everything seems louder than it used to be. Is that possible? Or are they just breaking me down, bit by bit? Their incessant clatter pounding, grinding in my ears. God have mercy on me, but if I were deaf nothing would ever disturb my dreams.

I have in my hand a postcard she sent me. It fell on the floor when the bookshelf exploded. What year was it she went to Portugal? She mailed a different card nearly every day. She must have loved me then. "Good friend" is such a depressing moniker. He is on the brink of experiencing everything, the whole of a person's heart, but in the end all he gets is a nice Christmas gift.

Once when we were leaving her house on a lovely spring evening, she said,

"You know, you and I are so much alike, but I like money more than you do."

"I could make a lot of money if I wanted to."

"You could make a lot of money, but it wouldn't mean anything to you. You'd just give it away. I'd buy all sorts of things with it. I like to surround myself with beautiful things, unusual things. That's why it would never work."

"What would never work?"

"Don't think about it now." And she kissed me lightly on the cheek and kept on walking.

Oh, to go back to that time! It's almost unimaginable now to think there were moments when she was actually next to me, talking to me, laughing at me, shaking her curly hair the way she did when she disagreed with something I said.

What would she think of me now? What do I look like compared to then? Women used to look at me when I walked down the street. But stop and talk to one of them? What was the point? They were all so common. "Do you like my shoes? They match my new hair color. I really like my job at the bank. I think I'll get my car painted red. How much money do you make a year? I don't like men with beards." No grace. No inner beauty. No charm. No intelligence. No sense.

But Helen. Helen. Those green eyes. I still find myself talking to her. Remembering. I would be tired, hungry, morose, broken down, but when I saw her, and she smiled, and we began the conversation, I came alive. Her lightning poured through me. Then I would become my best self. I became a being of worth as long as she was with me. When we parted, every single quality fell away, and I turned into this shabby, unnoticeable, miserable little creature clawing at the past.

But what else is there to do? Who has a suggestion? Is the better way to forget? Let her float away? Become like all the others?

There was the first time we went into the city together. How happy she was. She tried on every hat in that silly little store. Laughing. I thought I heard her laugh on the train the other day.

I could get married. That would help me forget. Yes, I know, Helen. She said I would never get married.

"You'll never get married."

"Why do you say that?"

"It would take a special woman to marry you."

"Of course she would be special. Do you think I would marry just anyone?"

"No, I mean you would require her to be so much. To know so much, so you could talk to her about everything. To be active, to be beautiful, to be sweet, to be kind, to be intelligent, witty, to take dreams seriously, to detach from the world and live with you in a sort of bubble, keeping out everything you think unimportant. There's no woman like that, outside of the ones in novels."

"Oh, I don't know." I was thinking of her, of course.

"You know I care about you. And I don't want to disappoint you. But how likely is it that you'll find her? In this world?"

"I have faith."

"I know you do. But is that enough?"

"What else do I need?"

"Faith is so hard. Some days I wake up, and I don't know if I have faith in anything. You know, that reminds me, I forgot to tell you about this man I met. I was walking near the university, and I stopped at the corner, and this man started talking to me. But he wasn't some slick operator trying to pick me up. He was young, and he had a gentle look in his eyes. He had long, really beautiful hair."

"Was he lost?"

"No, he didn't seem lost, but he wasn't from the city. He walked a few blocks with me. He talked softly. Sometimes I had to lean over to hear. It was almost like he didn't want to bother me, but, I don't know. It was strange but very sweet."

"Did he ask you out?"

"No. It wasn't about that. We talked about what was going on in the world. And you know what was weird? I felt so calm walking next to him. He left me and went into the coffee shop. He said he couldn't get used to the idea of flavored coffee."

I wanted the conversation to return to the topic of me.

"You know, I think about him," Helen said. Her green eyes flashed at me. "Maybe he was Jesus."

"Walking around the United States drinking coffee?"

"Why not? If He came back, where else would He go? You're always telling me how corrupt this country is. Doesn't it make sense?"

"Well, He certainly is needed here. But just because you met a coffee-drinking hippie doesn't mean Jesus has returned."

"Why not? Why can't I believe it? Why can't I have something concrete to believe in? If it helps me, what's wrong with it? If it gives me hope, what's wrong with it? You're the one who's supposed to have faith. Isn't it possible?"

Some days I'm so sick I can't get out of bed when I think of how I talked to her then. Always with the jokes. Being clever, being witty. Maybe that's why . . . If I had her in front of me now asking that question—just to see that face again. Isn't it possible? Every day, that's my prayer, Helen. Isn't it possible? Is it still possible? Please let it be possible. Every part of my being, the slightest breath when I'm asleep, lives so that one day it will be possible.

Perhaps I caused her too much pain. Perhaps I was the cause of her unhappiness and sorrow. If that is so, Lord, please punish me for it. I will accept whatever You decide. What am I saying? I'm here aren't I? In this place, day after day. What would be a worse fate? I have no fear of dying a violent death. My fear is waking up again tomorrow. I had an idea that I would sleep a few minutes more each day. By continuing to do this, I will soon be sleeping the entire twenty-four hours. A much greater possibility there will be to dream of her.

Remember the dream where she came up behind me and put her arms around me? I felt warm for days after that. Sometimes I dream of other women. I'm trying to keep pure, Helen. It's not my fault. During my waking hours I only think of you. I have kept my love strong every day. I've never wavered. I have not been with anyone else. I don't even look at women. They horrify me. None of their faces could ever match yours. I will never forget. It's hard work that you left me. I never thought I would be strong enough. Forgive me my weakness. I always meant well. My love has kept me alive. My love has kept me a prisoner. I don't blame you. I used to, but I was mad then. I'm so much more advanced now. I have trained my mind and my heart. I don't cry anymore. Because I'm happy, I truly am. I had you in my life. How many can say that? Some people never find anyone. Isn't that right? Aren't there people like that? Never-ending darkness for many, pinpricks of light for a few.

In those occasional moments of doubt and despair, I realize if you did come back, you would find me pathetic: a selfish, graying creature living in the shadows, hiding under the covers. My dream will never reject me. She will always love me. But what would you do? Could I walk again by your side among those people? Smiling, eating, listening to them talk? Couldn't we just stay inside? You only need me. Life on the inside is so much better. We'll have our food delivered. And I'll sing to you. I've made a list of all the things we could talk about. It will be just like it was. But this time you won't leave.

I know you want to be with someone who will love you every moment. No one else is like I am, so ready for you. Remember when I sent you the poetry in the mail, and you called and told me how much it meant to you? Would anyone else do that? Would anyone else know just what you needed? I'm not going anywhere. I'm right here, Helen. As many years as I have on this earth I will wait. I always laughed in the face of the people who told me to try to find someone else. Fools. They know nothing about love, or women. How could they understand something so far above them? Our love is blessed. Our love is sacred. Even though you are not here, there is a constant beam that carries me. It lifts me above everything. I have something to live for beyond how they want me to live. I know their purpose is to defeat me, bring me down to their level, stomp on the love and beauty I have guarded inside. That's why they constantly make noise. To break me down. To make me weak. Because they can never have what we have. Their minds are too small to comprehend such beauty. My mind can see beyond this mundane, meaningless world. I see through all their lies and evil. So make all the noise you want! Do you hear me? I will not go down. I will not become part of it. You are not real. My dream is real. Helen is not gone. She's never been more alive. Bang on my door. Break it in. You will not touch me. I am not alive to any of you. She is all I see. She is the only one I will listen to. What's that, Helen? Yes, soon it will be time to sleep. Perhaps tonight she will kiss me as I drift off. I know I've felt her there before. I mean no harm. Why shouldn't I have love? Just leave me here. Helen knows where to find me. Walk softly, darling. Don't let them know you've arrived. Sneak into my bed, and hold my head gently in your hands. I knew this time would come. Don't say anything. Put out the light, my love. Put out the light.

Only This Tenderness

"Would you like to go out sometime?"

Joshua rose from his chair as the woman prepared to leave.

"No. I think I'm done here."

She put her purse under her arm and walked off. He was left standing on the sidewalk watching her pale legs beneath the swishing skirt. When he could no longer see her, he sat down and put his hands around the cold glass. He lifted the glass and rubbed it along his forehead and down both sides of his face for want of a cool, soothing hand. When was the last time he felt love? People hurried by, oblivious of his existence. But there was a time, Joshua remembered. They had stopped in a farming community, but only for two nights. It had been a long ride in the van, and everyone was hungry. There was only one local restaurant. It didn't even have a name, just a small room with a concrete floor and tables with no cloths. Every eye turned to stare at them. A girl led them to a back room. They were served chicken soup with rice.

All of them ate in silence until two dark eyes peered around the doorway.

"Hola. ¿Como se llama?"

One of the women in the group spoke Spanish.

"Hola, chiquita. ¿Como se llama?"

The little imp giggled and ran away.

"Oh, she's shy. That's so cute."

The travelers continued with their meal when the little girl this time took a few steps into the room, hesitatingly.

"*Hola,* little one. Come in. How do you say 'Sit down?'"

"*Sientate.*"

"Ce-en-ta-te. Sit with us."

Joshua stopped eating and looked toward the child with the dark hair and the plaid dress. She smiled and ran to the chair next to his, climbed up, and sat down. She pulled on his sleeve and was saying something.

"What's she saying?"

"She wants to know if you like her dress."

"*Si. Es muy bonita. Me gusto mucho.*"

"*Te gusta?*" She pointed to the bows on her shoulders.

"*Si. Me gusta mucho. Bonita.*"

She leaned forward, put her head on the table, and looked up at him.

"It looks like you've found a friend."

Joshua just then remembered what was in his pocket. He reached in and slowly pulled something out.

"*Hola. Hola.* Look at me," he said in a funny voice.

She laughed and reached for his finger.

"*Hola. ¿Como se llama? ¿Como se llama?*"

"*Me llamo Yovanna,*" she cried, and she pulled the finger puppet from his hand. He helped her put it, on and she climbed off the chair and began running. "*Mama. Mama. Mira.*"

The girl came to clear the soup bowls, and Yovanna was right behind. She clamored up beside Joshua and put something in his hand.

"*¿Quien es?*"

She said something he couldn't understand.

"What's she saying?"

"She said, 'You know who that is.'"

"How would I know?" He took the plastic figurine and held it up to her. "*¿Quien es?*"

She made a sound of frustration. "*Es Coco Elephante.*"

"Who? *¿Quien?*"

"Coco Elephante!"

"Oh. Right. Sure. What am I supposed to do with him?"

"She wants you to play with her. She didn't go to anyone else."

The girl was talking to the puppet on her finger. Joshua walked the plastic soldier along the table. *"Yo soy Coco Elephante. Yo soy Coco Elephante."* As he did so, Yovanna took the puppet and knocked over the giant plastic man. She laughed. He did the same thing again, and again she knocked him down. Each time he changed the sound of his voice, and each time she laughed louder. *"Yo soy muerte. Yo soy muerte. Ahhh."* Everyone was laughing. It went on and on. She would never tire of the game and neither would he.

"Do you want something? Do you want something else?"

"No, I'm fine. We're playing."

"Sir, you spilled the rest of your drink. Do you want me to bring you another one? Or something else?"

"What? Another what? Oh, no. No, I'm fine. I'm sorry. I wasn't listening. I was just . . . I didn't realize. Yes, I'll have another one. Nice and cold. Nice and fresh and cold. By the way, you don't speak Spanish, do you? No, I guess you wouldn't. Yes, I'll have another one. Why not?"

The waitress went inside and left him staring up at the cloudless sky.

"It's hot today, isn't it?" Joshua asked the woman sitting at the table next to his.

She made no reply. At least a nod of the head, he thought. A smile. Some acknowledgement that he was alive. He could feel all his senses, everything he touched the world with, crawling back up into his body. Balling up. He slumped in his chair and put his hands in his pockets. Yes, he still had it. He had thought it was lost. Joshua rolled it between his fingers. The stone he found on the trip. Blessed by the shaman. Cool and smooth. He made a fist. "Invest me with your power," he beseeched it. "Take me from this nothingness." He squeezed hard and closed his eyes.

He felt a tugging on his shoulder. Yovanna was saying something. If only he had advanced past high school Spanish.

"She wants to show you something. She wants to know if you want to see her book from school."

"She's in school?"

"I guess its some sort of preschool. Go ahead, answer her."

"Si. Si." He patted her on the head.

She ran out of the room, one shoe untied.

"Don't fall! I hope she doesn't fall. These floors are solid concrete."

"She probably plays in here every day. But today she has a playmate."

Smiling, with shoes clomping on the floor, Yovanna returned with a thick book in her hands. Joshua helped her up into the chair, and she pushed the book in front of him.

"¿Te gusta?"

"Si."

She opened the heavy volume to a page in the middle and pointed.

"Si," he said.

She handed him a crayon and pointed again.

"I think she wants you to draw what's on the page."

"Draw? I'm no artist."

Yovanna kept pointing and looking up at him with dark serious eyes.

"Okay." He made a few lines on the page. *"Es mono. ¿Si?"*

She looked at the scribbles, cocked her head, peeked over at him, and then she smiled. *"Si. mono,"* she said grudgingly. She turned to another page. *"Eso."*

"This one?"

"Eso. Eso."

He did his best to draw a banana. *"Platano."*

"No." She shook her head. *"No es platano."*

"Si. Es platano."

The determined little girl pulled the crayon from his hand and made a slight adjustment to his picture. *"Es platano."* He had forgotten the stem.

While the dinner plates were cleared and first the coffee and then the dessert was served by the silent young women, Joshua attempted to draw everything in the book: fruit, flowers, animals, angels, planes, trains, and Santa Claus. Running out of examples, Yovanna pointed to a poster on the wall.

"You want me to draw that? Impossible." It was a map of the town. "I can't do that. *Es impossible.*"

But she knew better. He had drawn everything else. She ran to the other side of the room and tried to climb up on a chair to point out how easy it was. But the chair was unsteady, and it looked like she was about to fall. Joshua hurried over and grabbed her. He set her back down on the ground and smoothed her dress. She ran off to find a toy. His heart was beating quickly.

Pounding. Like the beat of that drummer. Leaving the concert the other night he had sat near the window on the train going home, and a young woman sat next to him. She said hello as she sat, so he began to talk to her. Joshua's heart, she must have heard it. Pounding. Drumming. He tried to think of words to say. He had to be funny. He had to smile. She must have been interested. He began to speak again. But she was already talking to the young man across the aisle. They were smiling and laughing. She never turned back once to look at him or to say good-bye as she was leaving the train. Couldn't she hear it? It was so loud. How could she not hear it? He couldn't touch her, couldn't reach out his hand across the void to make a tiny hole, a crack in the barrier. What would he need for that? Hands of bronze. Hands of marble. Monumental hands to hold his heart. "This is what I have to give. How can you look away? How can you not accept it? I would tear it out if I could. Rip it out. It brings me nothing but agony and pain. Nothing but pain."

He leaned over, his head hitting the edge of the table.

"Are you all right, sir?"

"Oh, I'm fine. Everything's fine," Joshua said. He struggled to lift his head.

"Maybe you had a little too much . . ."

"Oh, that's not the problem. That's not the problem. Say, are you sure you don't know any Spanish?"

She looked at him, wanting to laugh. But she didn't.

"I might know a word or two."

"Can you just say them for me?"

"Right now?"

"Yes. Whatever you know. Anything. Just say them. Say them."

"*Hasta manaña*. How's that?"

"*Hasta manaña*. That's good. That's good. That's fine. *Manaña. Manaña . . .*"

Yovanna was sad when they told her they had to leave. She stood in the middle of the room and started to sing.

"What's she singing?"

"I think she's making it up. She's singing 'Please don't go. Please don't go.'"

"Little one, we have to go. But we'll be back tomorrow. We're here tomorrow, right?"

"We'll be in this area tomorrow," the tour guide said. "We can come back here tomorrow night."

"We'll be here tomorrow. *Manaña*. We'll see you *manaña*.

She stopped singing and looked at Joshua.

Manaña. Es verdad."

She didn't move. She didn't speak. Her hands tugged at the ribbon on her dress.

Joshua bent down and kissed her on the forehead.

"*Manaña*. Okay?" he whispered.

Yovanna hugged him and ran out of the room.

The next day, no matter where they traveled, all he could do was think about her. In the mountains, on the trail, eating a sandwich while looking down on the grazing sheep, he wondered what he could bring her that would make her smile. As the sun was setting and they were heading back, he worried that he would have nothing for her. An old woman carrying a baby on her back approached them from the opposite direction. She held out intricate, hand-woven bracelets. "Ten *soles,* señor. Okay, for you, eight *soles.*" He chose a many-colored one and put it in his pocket. The trip back into town seemed so very long. He hoped she wouldn't go to sleep before they arrived.

The young woman in the restaurant recognized them from the night before. Was she Yovanna's mother? Sister? She had the same dark eyes. She sat them in the same room. They sat around the table in the same order. Joshua tried not to appear anxious. After all, she was only some little girl.

The soup came. Empty soup bowls were taken away. Still no Yovanna. She was asleep. Or sick. Or her mother mistakenly thought she had been a nuisance. Dinner arrived, the same chicken as the night before. Joshua ate disinterestedly, only pretending to listen to the conversation. Then he heard those footsteps ringing on the concrete. He turned toward the door.

She was pointing at him, saying something repeatedly and laughing. But she would not enter the room.

"What's she saying?"

"She's asking you why you have your jacket on."

"I'm cold. It's cold tonight. *Hace frio. Hace frio.*"

She was talking to him, but he did not understand.

"What's she saying now?"

"She says, 'Take your jacket off. Don't you know you're inside?'"

Yovanna ran up to him, poked him with her finger, and ran away.

"She's focused on you, Joshua."

He heard her return but pretended not to notice. He picked at his meat while she climbed up noisily on the chair next to his. Slowly he reached his hand into his pocket as she watched. When he pulled out the bracelet, she reached for it and almost fell onto the floor.

Joshua caught her, made her sit properly, and pushed the chair up close to the table.

"Hold out your arm."

He lifted her right arm gently. She held it in the air. Joshua began to wind the bracelet around her wrist, slow and easy, so it wasn't too tight. She followed each of his movements with eyes so big. He made sure all the bright colors were visible. He tied the two ends into a knot.

"*¿Te gusta?*"

With a smile she slid off the chair and went to each person at the table with her arm held out to show them.

"*¿Muy linda? ¿No?*"

Giggling, with her arm straight in front of her, she ran from the room.

"*Mama. Mama. Mira.*"

Everyone had finished their meal and there was talk of warm, soft beds when Yovanna came back with toys in her hand. She started playing on the floor and singing.

"She's singing again."

"It's the same song as last night. 'Please don't go. Don't go home.'"

"*¿Yovanna, tiene hermanos o hermanas?*"

"What did she say?"

"She said she has twenty-seven brothers and twenty-seven sisters."

"Maybe that's what they call each other in her class."

"It doesn't look like she has anyone to play with here."

"Except Joshua."

The bill was paid, and it was time to leave. Each one as they passed said good-bye to Yovanna. They gave her a kiss or patted her head. She didn't take much notice, continuing with the game. She was waiting for Joshua, and she looked up.

"*¿Manaña*?" she asked him.

He kissed the top of her head and kept walking. She saw him leaving, so she followed.

"*¿Manaña, si? Manaña.*

He walked out into the street and could hear her footsteps on the gravel behind him. He motioned for her to go back inside. But he hadn't answered her.

"*¿Manaña? ¿Manaña?*"

He didn't look back. He knew she would still be standing there, hands playing with the ribbon on her dress, waiting for someone who would never return.

"Sir? Sir. It's time, sir."

"Huh? What? Time for what? Time for what?"

"Sir, we're closing. It's time to go."

"You're doing what?"

"Closing. You have to go now, sir. You can come back tomorrow."

"Ah, tomorrow. Tomorrow. I can come back tomorrow. We can all do whatever we want tomorrow. Everything will all be fine tomorrow. Right?"

"You can come back and stay all day tomorrow if you'd like. But you have to go now. Please. I've been here all day, and I need to get home to my daughter."

"You have a daughter? What's her name?"

"Wanda."

"Does she like puppets?"

"All kids like puppets."

Joshua put his hand into the pocket of his jacket and found what he was looking for. He pulled it out and held it up for the waitress to see.

"Hold out your finger."

She did, and he fit the likeness of a smiling monkey over it.

"That's so cute," she said.

"Give that to your daughter. I think she'll like it."

"Thank you. You are so sweet. That's so nice . . ."

The girl's shoulders started to shake, and Joshua could see that she was crying.

"What's wrong?"

"Oh, it's nothing. You know, I work so hard," she said between sniffles. "I try to be nice to people. But people in the city don't really care. My legs hurt so much when I go home every night. Then I want to play with my daughter, but I'm so tired. Things cost so much. I'm always worried about money. It just seems to be the same every day. Relentless. Then you just do this little kind thing. It's not much, I know. It's just a tiny little puppet. But I see so little kindness. At least none of it directed at me. I just want to thank you. For thinking of us." She wiped the tears with the back of her hand. "I hope you do come back tomorrow."

Looking a bit embarrassed, she put her head down and went back inside. Joshua wanted to ask her, stop her. He didn't know her name.

"Well, there's always tomorrow."

He realized what he had said, and he ran into the restaurant searching for her.

A Shadow

It had been a long day. Standing on the platform he felt a heaviness, an inability to keep upright. He leaned back against the pole, closing his eyes. Sounds, voices were somewhere out there. The cool of the stone felt good against the back of his head. So many thoughts. If only, one by one, they could just pass through the lining of his skull and float away.

The announcement of the train's arrival startled him. He gathered his strength and watched as the others silently boarded. He followed slowly, and as he walked down the aisle of the crowded car he noticed no smiles. There was a seat in the back. As he sat, he was sure he recognized the woman behind him. He turned, but she made no sign of greeting.

The train began to move. He put his ticket in the slot. The idea occurred to him that he should attempt to start a conversation with the woman he thought he knew, just to hear another voice instead of his own. But what to say? How to start? Always uncertainty. The trembling in his hands. But he would do it. He would think of something funny. See if she laughed. As he wondered what the words should be, he shut his eyes, his head tilted toward the window and he fell asleep.

He woke in a panic; it was dark outside, and he didn't know how far he had gone. When he turned around the woman wasn't there, and as he looked back and forth, he saw the car was almost empty. He called out to a man across the aisle, asking him where they were. There was no answer. He didn't see a conductor. Was he even on the right train? He jumped up and hit his head on the luggage rack just as the voice on the speaker called his stop.

His heart began to beat more slowly as he got off and stood still beside the old brick station. People brushed by him. He felt so weak. When he finally started to move he had to think about every step, will his feet forward. The weight of his legs matched the sluggishness in his mind. He walked down the stairs and held tight to the railing, taking deep breaths of cold air.

Every store in the shopping center was still lit brightly. The different colors were so inviting, promising cheerfulness and comfort. He made his way across heavy traffic and found himself looking in at one of the windows. Attractive, well-made-up women wearing long coats and gloves were being ardently attended to by beautifully slim women who smiled and laughed and motioned with their pure white hands. Perhaps they would smile at him.

Inside the store the noise was deafening, high heels and voices and something they tried to pass off as music. He walked the aisles, looking for the comforting smiles. Shoppers hurried past him, loudly speaking to each other, ignoring him. Shop girls concentrated on the clothes they were folding as he asked his polite questions, never raising their eyes to his. Money was exchanged, satisfaction attained. Everything whirled around him. They all must keep busy. He wanted to run. He calmly asked to be let through, but no one heard. Could they please let him pass? Business went on. He summoned his strength and shoved, pushing back the gasping women, knocking over a display, making a baby cry and stumbling out onto the pavement as a girl passing by laughed.

The cold wind hit his face as he tried to zip his jacket. Something was stuck, and as he struggled and pulled he thought he heard someone call his name. He turned around, looked up and down the street, back and forth, straining to see someone he knew.

No one. *Wouldn't it be nice to meet a friend,* he thought. *To meet a friend while walking alone at night in the dark winter.* He or she would come up to him, touch him on the arm and say, "Are you hungry?" They would go to a place with a warm room. Perhaps a fireplace. They would sit and talk and enjoy and eat. The food always tastes better when there's a friendly face across the table. Maybe some wine. Music would be playing. Schubert. Everyone would be smiling, and no one would be cold.

He was finally able to close his jacket, but it brought him little relief. Weary of walking, he wanted to rest. He sat on a bench by a lamppost and pulled out of his pocket the letter he had written early that morning.

Father Emmanuel held the paper close to his eyes and read.

> *Dear Lord,*
>
> *Dear Lord it has come to this. Another day. Another day of despair has come and gone. And still we are waiting. Every day I wait for You, wait for a sign. Every day I pray for direction. I pray for grace. I call out but I hear nothing. We are here. You have left us here. Abandoned? They all come to me one by one, to ask, to find an answer. "When will it get better? When will my husband find a job?" And all I can say is, "Wait. Wait. In His time. It is His plan." "But help me to understand, Father." Help them! I can tell them nothing. I know nothing. You give me nothing. Every day I pray and every night ends like this. And every morning I wake again and try to believe in the promise of the new day. The day when all Your glory will be revealed. The day when all will rejoice in joy. For we will know. We will know what You know. Your reason. Your reason for the pain and suffering. Your reason*

> *for the confusion. For the darkness. For the loneliness. We just want to know. Something. Anything but this eternal night. Have faith. Have faith. Every day I wake up with less. Faith in what? The overwhelming nothingness? No Word. No beautiful vision. Idle minds can imagine all sorts of devastation. What am I supposed to keep telling them? How am I to keep them from losing their way? Humans need constant inspiration. I am running out. You can't keep feeding people nothingness and meaninglessness and expect them to continue to believe. Soon they will take to any crude pleasure to replace what You haven't given. I have little left to give. I am so tired, Lord. Tired of asking and waiting and hoping. They are all tired of me, too. What was I chosen for? To be made a fool of? Preaching about purity and beauty to people You have left stranded here in this hole? What are we waiting for? Why all these endless days and hours? Why can't we just come to You right now? Most of our time is spent so uselessly. We don't know our purpose, we wander and waste. Is this all our lives are to mean? I know I am speaking in an unworthy manner. Forgive me. Forgive me for my life. I need help, so much help. The light barely flickers. I am a useless, empty vessel. I should have been filled with the bliss of Heaven. But instead I am a coward, selfish and insignificant. I walk with sadness, ashamed of what I have become.*

The clouds drew a curtain over what had been a bright moon.

The priest put the paper in his pocket and looked upward. He saw nothing but darkness. He continued to stare, looking for something, hoping, not hearing the approaching footsteps.

A man with shuffling, scraping feet sat heavily at the other end of the bench and let out a loud sigh.

Father Emmanuel turned his head and saw two eyes fixed on him. He was not frightened. Any human contact was welcome. He tried to wiggle his frozen toes, waiting for his guest to speak.

"I just blew it all, man. I just blew it all."

The forlorn figure put his head in his hands.

"I had it. I had it all. Right there. All of it. And then they took it, just like that."

He slapped his hands together and let out a moan, pulling the brim of his cap down over his eyes.

"Can you believe it? That's how they get you. They set you up, they set you up, they make you feel big, and then WHAM! They take it all away. Can you believe it?"

"I can believe it," the priest said.

"You know what I'm talkin' about." All of his clothing was black, even his shoes. "I was only gonna play for a little. Just a little. Just to get enough. Now it's all gone. All gone."

He sat quietly for a minute or two, seemingly contemplating his bad luck. The priest noticed he wasn't wearing socks and his shoes were almost worn through.

"How much did you lose?"

"Well, I started out with twenty bucks. That's all I had. I was winnin', losin', winnin', losin'. I got it up to fifty and I was gonna quit. But then I figured, what the hell, the Lord'll let me win one more time. And I swear then that I was gonna quit. I swear it. But then they took it all. Damn!"

He took off his cap and rubbed his head hard as if trying to erase the memory. The bench started to shake as he rocked back and forth.

"That's how it goes. Right? Right, my friend?" There was no bitterness in his voice. His smile showed the few teeth he had left.

"Here. Why don't you take this?" Father Emmanuel opened his wallet and found one twenty dollar bill left. He placed it in the unsteady hand.

"Oh, man. Are you sure? Is this for real? This is such a blessing. I never expected to see any more money tonight. Are you sure now? The Lord does His work in many ways. He sure is looking out for me."

"Lucky you," the priest said.

"I'm lucky now."

The grateful man slid awkwardly across the bench and hugged the priest, and his breath smelled of beer. Father Emmanuel turned his head and closed his eyes until it was over.

"I can't believe it. You musta been sittin' here for a reason. Would you pray with me?"

"What?"

"Pray with me. Let's give thanks to the Lord for His blessings." He folded his hands and closed his eyes.

"By all means," the priest said. His collar was hidden beneath his jacket.

"Lord, as I walk along in this wicked world—and sometimes I am as wicked as the next man, I won't lie to You, Lord—but I try my best to be true to You. And You have sent to me this one true brother, who has befriended me in my time of need. You have not abandoned me in this cold world. Thank You for my blessing. And please bless my brother in whatever he does and give him the strength that he needs in this world of sin. For although we may be sinners, Lord, I know You love us all. Thank You. Amen."

The man in black had knelt on the sidewalk to deliver his prayer. Father Emmanuel watched him slowly rise.

"So, you believe in all of this?"

"Yes," said the man, smiling simply.

"No matter what? No matter what happens?"

"No matter what. See, to me, it's not something you think about. It's not something you decide with your mind. It's either in your heart or it's not."

The priest felt a chill run through his body. He stood, and as he did his companion hugged him again.

"God bless you," he whispered in his ear. The money could be seen sticking out of his hand. He shuffled away.

A horn sounded, and it was as if the priest suddenly became aware. The noise of the city was all around him. People were in a rush going home, going to concerts, going to dine with the one they loved. The world was spinning, but he was still.

Father Emmanuel could see the church in the distance. How easy it would be to walk through those doors again, to enter the handsome stone building whose graceful architecture he had pointed out to many a visitor, to enter his room and undress and pray and eat the simple meal and speak the words required.

How easy. But he was unable to move. He could find no reason or purpose. Not the cold. Not his weariness. Not the holy words. Not even the snow that began to fall. He watched as the white flakes started to gather on his clothing, little specks that sparkled in the lights as they descended. All the people moving more quickly, afraid of the tiny drops of ice, afraid of being out in the open without protection, away from their security and warmth, outside their circle of comfort.

The priest knew that, even if he took shelter by a fire, or at the altar, or in a prayer, or even in his bed, he still would be outside. He wished for an end. An end to thought, an end to futile supplication, an end to time that dragged him along mercilessly. To be able to lie down and be covered by snow, frozen, forgotten, smothered in whiteness.

As he looked up into the sky he heard a voice and saw a familiar face. It was not a vision but a memory of a teacher from the university. "Open your heart, my brothers. Open your heart and let everything, good and evil, dissolve in the fullness of your love. That is what you are here to learn. Not words, not rules, not customs. But how to let the love in your heart conquer all."

Father Emmanuel closed his eyes, and the face faded away. The snow had stopped. He put his hands in his pockets and began to walk.

"My heart is black."

In a few minutes he would be home. He had early mass in the morning.

Sweet Dreams

"Ellen, you know it's late. We talked about this. Now turn off your light and get into bed."

The little girl giggled as she shut the switch and hid under the covers. She sang a song and squirmed around enough to make the old bed creak and shake.

"Ellen."

"Yes, Daddy."

"What are you doing?"

"Nothing."

"It doesn't sound like nothing."

"Daddy, will you read me a story? You didn't read me a story tonight."

"It's late, Ellen."

"Daddy, you said you'd read me a story. You said you'd read me a story every night before bed. I can't go to sleep without a story. It doesn't have to be a long story. Just a good one."

Her father appeared in the doorway. Even in the darkness his figure was imposing. He stood with his hands in his pockets and no shoes on his feet. He yawned, obviously ready for bed.

"Daddy, I'm ready for the story."

"Who said I would be reading one?"

"You're already here. Just one story. Just one story."

Justin Johnson shook his head and laughed. Would he always do whatever she asked, even when she was much older?

"All right, pumpkin, one story."

"Yea, Daddy. Yea!"

"But I don't have a book with me."

"Make one up. You're smart."

"I'm not that smart at ten o'clock at night."

"How 'bout all those books you read? Don't you remember one of them? Tell me one of those stories."

"Well, they're not really stories for children . . ."

"I know, Daddy. I know. Tell me a story about the rain."

"The rain?"

"Yeah. Where does the rain come from? Why is it wet? Why does it rain sometimes when the sun is out? Why aren't the drops bigger, like, big as a potato?"

What a curious child. She remembered everything, each experience. Always asking, searching. She reminded him of someone.

"Come on, Daddy. Please. Tell me. Tell me."

"Okay. A story about the rain. Well, there once was a very wise man."

"What was his name?"

"His name was Seth. And he lived in a small quiet house in the woods. And every day the birds came to visit him, and the butterflies and the squirrels."

"And the moose?"

"No. There were no moose."

"Why not?"

"Because they didn't live around there. Now, he was a peaceful man who appreciated all he had been given in his life. He had no desire for anything other than what he had always known. He knew how to plant and grow different fruits and vegetables. He got his water from the stream and his strength from the sun."

"Where did he get his clothes?"

"His clothes, well . . ."

"Was he naked?" She giggled.

"Urn, he perhaps was naked. It was a simpler time."

"Miss Bergman says it's a sin to look at a naked man."

"How would she know? She's never seen one."

The father cleared his throat and began again.

"Okay. Back to the story. This simple man, Seth, never wasted time feeling sad or sorrowful. He had no books, no television, but he did not need them. He never killed an animal nor broke a flower off from its stem. He appreciated all. But you know what made him the happiest? The rain. When it rained he would run outside and dance and splash and hop on one foot in the puddles. He would roll back and forth in the wet grass, laughing and giggling. He would lie in the stream and feel the water gush over his shoulders and chest and down his body. In fact, the only time he ever came close to feeling sad was when the rain stopped. But he understood all the elements of nature had their purpose and place, and he was heartened by the return of the sun and how its rays made the droplets on the leaves sparkle."

"Daddy, was he a wuss?"

"Now where did you ever hear that word?"

"Tina Smith says that people who don't hunt animals and who never step on bugs are wusses."

"Listen, Ellen," he said softly. "Do you want to hear the story? You keep interrupting and I may forget . . ."

"I'm sorry, Daddy. Keep going. I like it."

"All right." He scratched his head. "So, many years passed, and Seth was now very old. He knew he soon would be leaving this world. He had been blessed with a wonderful life, and for that he was grateful. He wanted to take pleasure in all that surrounded him as he always had, but he could not escape the thought that soon his eyes and ears and hands would no longer experience earthly beauty. What would happen when he ceased to be a part of all he had known?

"Every day he moved a bit more slowly, and every day he grew gloomier. None of the old pleasures seemed to inspire him. He had but one wish. He stumbled out of his house and called out to the sky to send him one more glorious rain.

"But every day there was only sun, boiling heat that drenched him in sweat and burned his feet, for he had no shoes. One day the sky grew dark, and the sun hid away, and he ran and tumbled over and crawled to the softest grass, and he opened his mouth and held out his hands, but only four drops fell before the blue sky returned. Too tired to curse his fate, he headed home.

"Then came the day when his heart had almost stopped beating, and he knew it would be his last. He said good-bye to his house and his few possessions, and he made his way through the woods to the stream. The water was cold at first, but soon its rhythm became his own. He closed his eyes and imagined he was not in one place, but everywhere the water floated and swam and crashed and sank and flooded and drenched and whirlpooled or lay in stillness.

"Then, suddenly, a loud explosion shook the forest. Animals began scurrying, and the leaves flew by on a raging wind. Seth heard it before he felt it lightly hitting the trees, not having much weight, suspended above, then slowly growing, accumulating, getting heavier, coming faster, louder and louder, harder and harder, until the trees were useless, and everything fell through, and his skin was alive with the sting of it, blinding him, bathing him, soothing him, drowning him. Wonderful rain.

"Joyful one last time, he was overwhelmed with thankfulness. It was time, and he died with a happy and contented soul. And as the rain ended and the earth warmed, the cycle began again. Water falls from the sky and flows into the ground until the clouds call it back and then let it go again. But there has been one difference since that day. Every time the rain lulls you gently to sleep, every time a thunderstorm makes your heart race with fright, every time the roots of the trees hungrily drink, every time a summer shower cools your face, and even when the snow leaves a glistening blanket of beauty, the old man is there, laughing with you, singing with you, in every drop, in every snowflake, bringing you joy and easing your pain.

"And that is the story of the rain."

"Wow, Daddy, that was a good one." The little girl yawned. "Did you make that up yourself?"

"All right, Ellen, those are enough questions. It's time to go to sleep."

The weary father got his daughter to lie down and made sure her favorite stuffed animals were also tucked in.

"Daddy, will I ever see the old man?"

"Maybe if you close your eyes and try, you can see him."

"Like we can see Mommy?"

"Yes, darling."

Mr. Johnson brushed the hair away from his daughter's forehead and kissed her twice. He walked softly into the hall, but she was not asleep.

"Daddy, I wish it was like you said it used to be when they didn't let ladies fight in the war."

"So do I, my love."

He left the door open so he could hear her call.